The bush behind D[...]

he thought, remembering the grin on Paddy's face. But it didn't sound like a duck, or a fox either, come to that. He raised his hand and started to click his fingers, but then thought better of it.

The bush rattled again. He turned and peered into the shadows. Something was moving in there, black on black, too big to be an animal.

Stay together. Tony had warned him.

To hell with it.

He hefted his baton, then turned and pushed his way between the overhanging branches. Something white was moving in there.

He saw them at the same time as they saw him. The older lad raised his hand. Moonlight flashed on dull metal.

A gun. Dave registered it and had his hands in the air in the same heartbeat. . . .

SOLDIER
SOLDIER

TUCKER'S STORY

by Sarah Jackson

CENTRAL

B⬛XTREE

First published in Britain in 1995 by
Boxtree Limited,
Broadwall House, 21 Broadwall, London SE1 9PL.

10 9 8 7 6 5 4 3 2 1

Cover photographs by Central ITV show Rosie Rowell as
Donna Tucker and Robson Green as Fusilier Dave Tucker

Typeset in Sabon by SX Composing Ltd, Rayleigh, Essex
Printed and bound in Great Britain by
Cox & Wyman Ltd, Reading, Berkshire

ISBN: 0 7522 0750 4

A CIP catalogue record for this book is available from
the British Library

Acknowledgements

Thanks to:
Ben Jeapes, Tristan Kirby, Jay Knox-Crichton and
Andy Lane for all the help – though all errors and sins
of omission are mine alone. Thanks also to all the
usual suspects for all the usual reasons – you know
who you are.

Prologue

Dave Tucker slapped the pan of vegetables down, and hitched himself up on to the table next to it. Outdoor cooking was something he was used to. Good at, even. It was hardly surprising. He did a lot of it.

It was always the same. Today was a good example. Here they were, crashing round the Welsh mountains on training, but as soon as anything important needed doing, what did he get? Stay here and make dinner, Tucker.

Never mind that he wanted to be off with the others, searching for the chopper that had gone down with Colonel Fortune, the padre and a couple of other men aboard.

Join the army. See the world.

Join the army. Do what you're told.

Still, it could be worse. He glanced at Rachel Elliot, the lady journalist who'd come with them for the day. She was sitting near the table. That was why he had moved – so he could cheer her up. She looked as miserable as sin, wrapped up in scarves and a donkey jacket against the biting mountain air.

'Soon have some grub inside you,' he said. Best thing for her. He picked a potato out of the box and started peeling it.

'I'm fine,' she said, though the wind whipped her words away. 'I suppose they have got things on the helicopter?'

'Everything,' Tucker said, relieved he could answer honestly. 'First aid, food, drink . . . they've even got the Bible basher with them.' Damn, he thought. It might not have been the most tactful thing to say. As Donna was always telling him, he'd try to cheer a dying man up because he felt sorry for him – by telling him he was sure to go to heaven.

'Poor Simon,' Miss Elliot said. 'It would happen to him.'

First names? Tucker wondered. He supposed you would be on first-name terms if you were a pretty lady journalist up from London.

'Helicopters? Never trust them,' he said, and thought, bloody hell, there I go again. 'What I say is, if we needed that sort of thing, we'd have joined the Air Corps.' He stopped peeling and jabbed his knife at her recorder. 'You can tell them that.'

'I don't know what I'll be telling them,' she said. 'It depends on what happens.' She sounded distracted. Worried about her article, is she? Tucker wondered. Or worried about something else – like the Colonel?

Best if she didn't dwell on it, he decided. 'Still, whatever you write, you won't be doing me, will you?'

'Oh, won't I?' she asked.

She was pretty enough, with the wind whipping pink into her fine skin. Out of his class, mind; and anyway, not a patch on his Donna.

'Like they didn't pick me for the search parties,' Tucker said. He found an eye in the potato, and dug the knife in hard to get it out. 'Never mind!' He sounded right pissed off about it – which he was. He just hadn't meant to let it show so much.

'Perhaps they didn't know you wanted to be picked,' Miss Elliot said.

Like bloody hell. 'When I first joined up, Colonel Fortune was a major. Belfast.' He scraped hard at the potato. Keep this up and there wouldn't be any spud left, only scrapings. But he kept at it anyway. 'I was his runner. Eighteen, I was, and spotty.' He grinned at Miss Elliot, and she smiled back. 'Had this bastard of a CSM. He gave me all sorts of grief. But the Old Man?' He tossed the potato into the pan and picked out another one. 'He was all right.' Best you could ever say about the army, really. And now he might be lying out there somewhere, injured. And what was Dave Tucker doing to help? Peeling bloody potatoes. 'Wouldn't have minded going.'

A little later – not long, though it felt like hours, with still no word – Tucker took a break and made some tea. Midnight Rawlings came out of the radio tent to join him. There was no need to ask if there was any news: the grin on his face said it all.

Miss Elliot hurried across the grass towards them, obviously having trouble keeping up with Tony Wilton, who was holding forth about something or other.

'We'll have them out of there in minutes,' Wilton

9

said as they came within earshot. Tucker had heard recruitment adverts that sounded less gung ho. Good old Tony, Tucker thought. He'd never been the same since he got his third stripe.

'Yes, I'm sure,' Miss Elliot said. She sounded as if she'd had enough of his spiel, so Tucker was glad when he went off to check on something very urgent on the other side of the encampment – like, someone who'd tied their shoelaces against regulations. God forbid Wilton should let anything slide.

'What's he going on about?' Tucker asked. He handed Miss Elliot a mug. She wrapped her hands round it. The steam curled up into the chilly air. 'The A-Team to the rescue, I suppose?'

'Four blokes down, no rescue services in sight and he's still singing "Land of Hope and Glory",' Midnight said. He took a drag on his cigarette. His orange windcheater was vivid against his black skin, and it crackled as he moved.

Tucker held his mug in both hands, glad of the warmth. 'I just get pissed off,' he said. He'd given up pretending he wasn't. 'Major Cadman's gone, and we've got this new bloke – he's Scottish. My mate gets promoted and it's like having a jar with an RSM.' He slurped his tea. 'Tony Wilton gets made sergeant and he's a five-star general.'

'Hitler,' Midnight agreed.

Tucker sighed and stared at his tea. He glanced at Midnight. 'Everyone's moving up but us.'

Miss Elliot grinned. 'So what's stopping you?' she demanded.

Journalists, Tucker thought. Get him started on that and they'd be there all day.

'I've only been in five minutes,' Midnight said. He sounded affronted. He gestured at Tucker with his mug. 'He's the one you should ask, sweetheart.' He headed round the back of Tucker, back towards the radio tent.

Rachel looked inquiringly at Tucker. He could tell her the truth – tell her about his court martial, all of that. But if he'd learned one thing from it, it was not to blame others. Besides, he wouldn't want to wake up and find it all over the newspapers.

'Me? I don't need to be stopped,' he said. He sniffed, and headed round to the far side of the table, to get ready for dishing up. 'No use blaming the other sods. Army's full of moaners.' Miss Elliot twisted round to follow him, and he realized she needed someone to talk to. Well, the stew wouldn't be ready for a while yet. He came round her other side, and leaned against the table next to her. 'If it wasn't for the army, I'd be driving a BMW, me,' he said.

She laughed. 'Oh, it's that good, is it?' she asked. She sounded a bit embarrassed. Probably drives one herself, Tucker thought.

'There's worse,' Tucker said. He was suddenly struck by a memory of Newcastle town centre on a rainy Tuesday afternoon. He should have been at school, but he couldn't be bothered. He'd peered into the job centre and seen half-a-dozen lads from the year before his, all standing around looking at the couple of cards on display. 'The dole. Factories. All that.'

'You really are keen, aren't you?'

'Give over – someone might hear,' Tucker said. Miss Elliot grinned. 'Yeah,' he said. 'They're a good mob. But then we've got a good CO.' That pleased her. 'Needs a wife,' he said, testing.

She looked sharply at him. 'So do I,' she said after a minute. She was laughing, but only just. 'Someone to shop, clean, peg out my washing.'

Tucker took a long, long drink of tea. She was soft on the Old Man, then. Well, he could do a lot worse. So could she. 'His first wife died.' He looked straight at Miss Elliot. She looked back at him, her face unreadable, so that he couldn't tell whether she'd known or not. 'She'd been sick for a bit. He looked after her.' Christ man, Dave, he thought to himself. You're supposed to be cheering her up, not dragging her down. 'I'm married,' he said. 'Donna.' He couldn't keep the pride out of his voice. Sometimes he wondered what he'd done to deserve her – good or bad. But just now even the thought of her was enough to cheer him up. 'She's a real stunner.'

'Is she army barmy, too?'

'Drives her barmy,' Tucker said. It was the one thing that always got between them. 'She hates it.' He stared sadly at Miss Elliot. That was the trouble with trouble, he thought. No matter how you tried to forget it, it always brought you down. And if you were in the army – or married to it – trouble was never too far away. 'Forget all this crap about marrying the army. You go for the bloke like he goes for the girl.' He paused for a second. 'Trouble is, I'm already taken.'

And then she really did laugh.

Chapter 1

Donna Tucker stared at the photo of the block of flats pinned to the wall. It looked like every other block of flats she'd ever seen – the only difference was the startling blue of the sky above it. The label underneath it said *Married Quarters*.

Hong Kong, she thought. Bloody hell. Dave might as well be posted to Gateshead by the look of those flats.

The battalion had put this display on for the wives. They did it before every posting, to let them see what they were in for. Donna reckoned the best bit of it was the free wine. She already knew what she thought about Hong Kong.

She tapped the photo with her finger. 'Don't think much of that,' she said. She turned and grinned at her friend Nancy. Then she noticed the picture next to it: an Olympic-size outdoor swimming pool. 'But I could hack a bit of that, eh Nance?'

Nancy grinned. She was a Redcap, and if anything she was having a worse time with the whole idea of the Fusiliers moving to Hong Kong than Donna was. 'So could I, given half the chance,' she said. She was going out with Paddy Garvey, a Corporal in Dave's platoon – and girlfriends weren't required on the trip. 'Which I won't be, of course,' she added bitterly.

Before Donna could answer, Major Cochrane came in. He leaned against the door jamb and grinned at them.

'Is it true what they say about Hong Kong night life, Major?' Donna asked. Pubs, clubs, sun, sand and sea. Sounded all right to her, and no mistake.

'Better be,' he said. He came over. 'Small compensation for manning the last outpost of Empire.' Donna stared at him. She could put up with her Dave liking the army life – it was a good life for a lad, after all – but the Major was over the top. Every time he opened his mouth he sounded like he was auditioning to take part in a recruiting advert. 'Oh, it's a life of sacrifice,' he finished, and Donna realized he'd been joking all along.

She chewed her gum. It had long since lost its flavour, but she couldn't see anywhere to get rid of it. 'Oh aye,' she sighed, thinking of hot sun, white beaches and late nights out.

Nancy smoothed down the bottom of her uniform jacket. 'I don't suppose you've got any room for girl-friends, have you, sir?' she asked. You had to admire her for trying, Donna thought, though they all knew the answer.

'Taking girls to Hong Kong? Bit like taking coals to Newcastle.' Major Cochrane paused. Here we go, Donna thought. She stared at the display screen. 'Eh, Mrs Tucker?' he finished.

Who's a clever boy, then? Donna thought. She flashed him her sweetest smile. 'I wouldn't know,' she said. 'We always had gas at home.'

Major Cochrane smiled at her uncertainly, as if he knew she was taking the piss but didn't know how to handle it. Then he turned and left.

Nancy made to follow him, as if she were going to try and get a different answer to the question she'd just asked. Bad mistake, Donna thought, especially with her being as near as in the army as made no difference.

'Give over moping, Nance,' Donna said. She gestured extravagantly at the display board. 'You can fly out on holidays.'

Nancy stared at the floor. 'I wouldn't want to spoil his fun,' she muttered. She glowered at Donna. 'He won't be a monk for two years, will he? Not the testosterone kid.'

No point getting pissed off with me, pet, Donna thought. Then again, she wouldn't have trusted Dave alone in Hong Kong for two minutes, let alone two years.

'The stupid thing is, a couple of months back it was him wanting to get wed and me doing the "let's not rush into it" routine,' Nancy said. She headed towards the door again, and this time Donna followed her. 'I made him promise not to ask me again.'

'Well, you've changed your mind,' Donna said. Nancy was a bright lass, but sometimes she couldn't see straight ahead of her. 'Just tell him.' Anyone would think it was a big problem, but Donna knew how to deal with men – you told them what you wanted, and after you'd said it enough times, the poor wee lads got the idea.

16

'Oh yeah,' Nancy said. 'Me propose to macho man. He's going to love that.'

Idiot, Donna thought. 'Look, just wed the pillock,' she said with barely concealed exasperation. 'Then they'll post you over there as well.'

'Yeah, but –' Yeah but, yeah but, Donna thought. Anyone would think Paddy Garvey had some say in the matter. 'You don't know what he's like, Donna. If I pop the question to him, I won't see him for dust.'

There was no telling some people, Donna decided: men were all the same – little boys waiting for a woman to tell them what to do next. 'Oh give over, Nance.' Donna waved her information sheet in the air. 'I tell you – get your finger out before it's too late.' She marched off.

'I do know, Donna,' Nancy said from behind her.

Donna grinned. She was a good lass, Nancy. She'd get the message sooner or later.

One little mistake, Dave Tucker thought, one little mistake and they never let you forget it. He was waiting next to the model table in the Tactics Room with the rest of the platoon. Bollocking time, Dave thought. It was only a practical joke they'd played on Marilyn – real name Monroe, which was irresistible – the new recruit, but it had buggered up the rest of the training exercise. And Tony Wilton might be a mate, but he was like a cat with a can tied to his tail if they didn't turn in a top-notch performance.

Dave picked up the pointer and pretended to line up a pool shot – bam, and he'd pot the church steeple straight into the side pocket.

Paddy Garvey came in, talking to Marilyn. Telling him not to be so wet, if Dave knew Paddy. Good man, Paddy.

The next shot would be tricky – a rebound off the cushion would let him pot the red pick-up truck into the top pocket, or –

Paddy grabbed the pointer. 'Come on, Sarge,' he yelled. 'Some of us have got beautiful women waiting for us.'

'Yep,' Dave said. 'But she's not going to wait for ever.' He grinned.

'No, she won't,' Midnight said from beside him.

Paddy rubbed the black camouflage on his face with the side of his thumb. 'That's not my fault,' he said stiffly. 'I kept on asking her, she kept on saying no. She'll never get wed.'

Poor Paddy, Dave thought. Didn't have any idea how to deal with women. They thought they were smart: you just had to be smarter. 'Course she will,' he said firmly.

'Course,' Midnight agreed.

'You know what your trouble is? You've always courted her,' Dave continued. Well, he thought, not so much courting her as running after her like a cat after a fishmonger's van. 'Should be the other way round.'

'The other way,' Midnight put in. 'You try too hard, corp. Play hard to get.'

'Frankly, my dear, I don't give a damn,' Dave said, in his best Erroll Flynn voice. Or should that be Clarke Gable? One of them, anyway. He sniffed. 'A

18

bit off hand and she will be begging you for that ring,'
he said firmly. He stared at the table. 'Worked for
me,' he added. Well, not strictly speaking – he'd had
to promise Donna the earth, the moon and the stars
above before she said yes. But in principle he was
right.

'And for me,' Midnight said. 'Hold up,' he said.

Wilton came into the room. Back to business, Dave
thought.

Nancy walked into Joy Wilton's flat just as Donna
finished her third cup of tea of the afternoon. She had
a carrier bag in one hand, a box from the baker's in
the other, and a grin on her face so wide it was
amazing her head didn't split in half.

'Cheerful today, aren't we?' Donna asked. She
winked at Joy.

Nancy marched over to where they were sitting,
and plonked the cake-box on the table. Then she
pulled a bottle of wine out of the carrier bag, and
said, 'Got a corkscrew, Joy?'

'I'll get some glasses,' Donna put in. She nudged
Joy in the ribs.

'What are we celebrating, anyway?' Joy asked, in
her best innocent voice. She did it very well.

Nancy started to sing, 'I'm getting married in the
morning, ding dong the bells are gonna chime – '

Joy grabbed Nancy and hugged her till she had to
stop singing. Then it was Donna's turn, while Joy
scurried off to find the corkscrew and some glasses.

'Let me look at you,' she said, holding the smaller

woman at arm's length. 'What did I tell you? Didn't I tell you it would be all right?'

There was a loud pop from behind them. Joy handed out the wine.

Nancy held her glass up and the wine fizzed gently. 'The local's best sparkly stuff,' she said. 'To Hong Kong.'

Donna sipped her drink. It tasted like cat's pee gone off. 'So Nancy – are you going tell us who asked who, or do we have to guess?' she asked.

'That's for me to know and you lot to get out of Paddy – if you can,' she said, and laughed.

'Dave?' Donna said. She rolled over in bed. Next to her, Dave seemed hardly more than a pale heap of bedclothes in the darkness. Donna reached under the quilt and put her arm round him. Dave grunted. He'd had a long hard day's training, and it was no wonder the poor lamb was tired, she thought.

'Gerroff, Donna,' he said.

'Come on, Dave. Tell us.'

Dave rolled over. 'What?'

'You know.'

'I don't. Now leave us alone, I've got to be up early in the morning.'

Donna reached down and squeezed a *very* delicate part of Dave's anatomy. Dave yelped.

'Tell us then – did you talk Paddy into proposing to Nancy?'

'That'd be telling.'

Donna squeezed again. Harder.

'Ow! You little – '

Donna grinned and did it again. 'Plenty more where that came from, sunshine.'

Dave reached for her. She rolled back, out of the way.

'All right,' he said. 'I'll tell you. Just promise you won't – ' He caught his breath. 'Won't – '

Donna grabbed him. 'Won't what?'

'Stop,' he said.

Donna let him go. 'Did you?'

'Yes!' he said. 'Now get yourself over here – '

'I thought you were tired,' Donna said sweetly.

Donna put a cup of tea down in front of Joy Wilton.

'Thanks,' Joy said. Donna had invited her round to get the low-down on what happened when they moved out. 'Right,' she said, once Donna had sat down. 'The Accommodation Officer will go through the inventory. Anything that's left dirty or damaged, they'll fine you.'

Donna stared at Joy. She couldn't believe what she was hearing. 'You're joking,' she said. Joy stared at her calmly. Well it was all right for her, Donna thought. She was used to the army – had to be, married to Tony look-at-me-I'm-a Sergeant Wilton. 'You'll be all right then,' she said. It wasn't that she didn't like the other woman, but sometimes she was just so prim and proper it got right on Donna's wick. 'Top marks, Mrs Wilton. Let me kiss your bottom – ' She'd gone too far. She couldn't look Joy in the eye, so she stared at the wall.

'Donna, you asked me what happens when you're marched out – ' Marched out, Donna thought. That was just army-speak for moving to Hong Kong. Like they were going to carry all their worldly goods in a knapsack on their backs. 'I don't mind helping first-timers, but if you don't want to know – '

She was right, Donna realized. There was no point screaming at her when it was the army she was pissed off at. 'Aah, you get better treatment from the bailiffs,' she said. 'I didn't ask to go to Hong Kong.'

'The whole battalion goes through it, not just you – ' Yeah, yeah, Donna thought. That just made the whole battalion soft, as far as she was concerned. ' – And if you want to get off to Newcastle first, you're – '

'Newcastle?' Donna said. What the bloody hell had put that into Joy's head. She started to say as much, but at that moment Nancy came in.

She had a face as miserable as a wet weekend in Bognor, and she dragged herself towards the kitchen. 'Mind if I make some coffee?' she asked as she passed the room divider.

If that's how she sounds when she's on her way to her own wedding, Donna thought, I'd hate to see her get ready for a funeral.

'Everything okay, Nance?' Joy asked.

'Yeah,' Nancy said. She stared first at Joy, then at Donna. 'No,' she admitted. 'I don't know.' She leaned on the counter top. 'I mean, I feel like I've been hijacked by this big ape swinging down from the trees.'

Donna snorted. 'Sounds all right to me,' she said.

She could have done with a bit of the ape-man routine from Dave – but these days he seemed to use up all his energy mucking around harassing poor little new recruits.

In Dave's considered opinion, Marilyn's problem was that he was far too easy to wind up. Took all of the challenge and some of the fun out of it.

Not that Dave was going to let that stop him. Midnight didn't quite see it that way, though. He said as much when Dave told him about the latest trick he had prepared. They were taking some bits of lumber into one of the houses mocked up on the exercise ground.

'Why not?' Dave demanded.

'Enough's enough,' Midnight said. He glanced across the yard, to where Tony Wilton was briefing Paddy Garvey.

So that's it, Dave thought: he's worried about what the Old Man'll say. Still wet behind the ears, that was Midnight's trouble.

'It works lovely,' he said, and added soothingly, 'It won't hurt him, I promise.'

'You're going to owe him a drink after this, you know that?' Midnight said as they got to the house.

Yeah, yeah, Dave thought. Well, if Marilyn had come down the boozer a bit more often, maybe they wouldn't have been so tempted to wind him up all the time.

He hurried inside after Midnight, and closed the

door just as Marilyn went past. Inside, he'd suspended a huge sharpened stake on a rope, and rigged it halfway up the stairs.

Well, he thought, the sign on the door did *say* 'Booby traps'. Not that this was anything like what the brass had in mind. He set the unwieldy sheet of chipboard he was carrying down, and went over to the rope that would set the stake free.

'Where is he?' he muttered. If Garvey or Wilton – or worse, God help them, Major Cochrane – came in, they'd be up shit creek for a week. 'Monroe!' he screamed. 'You should be in here! Now!'

The door opened. Monroe came in and turned to close the door behind him.

'Look out, Marilyn,' yelled Dave, and tugged on the string. Monroe turned. The stake hurtled towards him. He jerked his hands up to protect himself, with an expression of absolute terror on his face. He screamed and turned aside with his hands over his head as the stake slammed to a halt six inches from him.

Dave cawed with laughter. It was the best yet, the very best. The expression on the kid's face . . . Dave couldn't hold it in: he found that he was doing a little tap dance round the hallway.

'You all right?' he heard Midnight ask. He helped Monroe to a seat on the stairs.

Of course he was all right, Dave thought. He'd never been in any danger, but the expression on his face – that had been worth six months' pay.

'You stupid bastard,' Midnight said. Too close to

his own welcome to the army, that's his trouble, Dave thought. Any minute now he'd have to slip out and take a leak, he was laughing so hard.

The door banged open. Paddy Garvey appeared, his huge frame almost filling the whole doorway. 'What the hell is happening in here?' he hissed.

'Jimmy's had a bit of a scare,' Midnight said. He stared at Dave as if daring him to say anything about it – as if he thought he'd land Marilyn in it. Bloody cheek.

Paddy kicked the door shut. 'I might have known. First bloody balls-up it would be you.' He leaned down and stuck his face close to Marilyn's. 'Shall I tell you something, Fusilier – '

Whoops, Dave thought. It was one thing putting the wind up the little bugger; quite another to let him take a bollocking for it. 'I'm sorry, Corp,' he said; but he suddenly remembered the look of terror on Marilyn's face when he saw the stake, and it set him off laughing again. 'It was my fault,' he finished through his giggles.

Then Marilyn blew it. He got up and started to walk away.

Paddy grabbed him by the arm and swung him round, then pinioned him up against the wall. Dave headed out of the door: if Paddy was going to do anything he shouldn't, Dave wanted to be able to say he hadn't seen it.

Behind him, Paddy said, 'Do you want me to get physical?'

'Leave me alone,' Marilyn screamed. Dave turned,

just in time to see the recruit ram Paddy against the far wall. 'Leave me alone, leave me alone,' he shouted.

He pushed past Dave and ran full tilt across the square.

'Oy Jim!' Midnight shouted. 'Don't go. It was only a joke!'

Yeah, Dave thought. Tell that to Tony Wilton. Or Major Cochrane.

Later on – after Tony Wilton had had one of his little words with them – the platoon ran out to muster in the exercise ground. A couple of the other lads brought Marilyn along with them.

'I don't want you going near him,' Wilton had said, when Dave offered to go and fetch him back.

Typical, Dave thought. Bloody typical. You try to do your bit to help, and what do you get? A flea in your ear.

'Keep those guns up,' Wilton yelled as Dave ran past him. Not to worry. It would all blow over.

They came to a halt and formed up into a square, cradling their yellow-barrelled rifles in their arms. Major Cochrane strolled round in front of them, closely followed by Tony Wilton. 'Okay, lads?' the Major asked. 'Over at the live firing area tomorrow. What's the verdict so far, Sergeant Wilton?'

Wilton paused next to Dave and Midnight. He clutched his clipboard like it was stuck to his chest. 'Could be better, sir,' he said. 'But we'll be over in that lecture-room next week, and we'll be going over every single inch of it.'

26

Give us a break, Dave thought. He caught sight of Paddy. 'Corporal Garvey's going to be going over every single inch of something else, sir.' He jabbed his rifle barrel in the air.

'Know what I mean,' Midnight sniggered.

Cochrane didn't rise to the bait. 'You managed to get booked up then, Corporal?' he asked as Paddy took his place beside him.

'Day after tomorrow, Sir. Twelve o'clock,' he said. 'She's picking her dress right now.'

'You right for a few jars tonight?' Dave asked. A few of the lads agreed, but Major Cochrane seemed surprised he was asking. 'As best man, you know,' Dave said by way of explanation.

'He's not, is he?' Midnight asked.

'Oh my giddy aunt,' Wilton said, grinning.

Well, that's charming that is, Dave thought.

'Yeah, I suppose so,' Paddy said.

The Major strode away. 'If Tucker's the best, God help the rest,' he said as he went.

Nancy looked a real picture in the dress she'd picked out. Princess Diana couldn't hold a candle to her – not with all that lace, and those frills.

Not that it was Donna's kind of thing, mind you. She much preferred the silk suit she had chosen.

'I felt sexier in my jeans,' Nancy moaned.

'We're not supposed to look sexy,' Joy chided. 'We're supposed to look pure.' She held up a hank of Nancy's hair to see how it would look tied up.

Stuff pure, Donna thought. She slid in front of Nancy to look at herself in the mirror.

That night, Dave and Tony took Paddy out to get him rat-arsed. What was the point of getting married, if you couldn't get pissed with your mates first?

Nancy turned up halfway through. She was in uniform, and she had her hair pulled back tight in a bun. At least, Dave thought she did. By that time he was a bit too squiffy to see straight, and all he really knew was that she pulled Paddy away from his rightful piss-up and insisted on talking seriously. By that time, Dave was in a black wig, tight dress and a pair of stilettos – well, you couldn't do the Supremes impersonation without them – and when he and Tony made a raid to get Paddy back, she screamed at him to grow up.

Donna was busy cleaning and scrubbing and washing, all under Joy's direction. You'd have thought the bloody flat was an operating theatre, not a home, the way she went on.

Then Nancy turned up in a right state. Joy brought her in, calmed her down and gave her a cup of tea, but she still sat there with a face like a wet weekend.

Well, she'd just have to get on with it. Donna had a floor to clean. She sprayed the stuff Joy had given her on the vinyl, then set to rubbing it. 'Great, isn't it?' She said. 'We get shunted all round the world and who gets lumbered with all the work? Not the flaming men, I can tell you.'

'Some of them do their fair share,' Joy said. She was a right little madam at times, Donna decided, always going on about what a perfect gem her army-barmy little Napoleon of a husband was. 'Right,' Joy went on, getting ready to make another one of her lists. 'Flowers for the wedding – '

'Aye. But not mine,' Donna said belatedly. 'Still, better a happy slob than a psycho in uniform – '

'I hope you're not referring to my Tony,' Joy said.

Course I am, pet, Donna thought; but what she said was, 'Thirteen-thirty hours, they said.' She went into the kitchen to start the cupboards. 'Why they can't just say dinner time . . .' They looked all right to her, but she knew Joy would say different. 'For all they know I might have something important to do the morrow,' she shouted through.

'Stop it, Donna,' Joy said. Donna heard her say something to Nancy quietly.

More bloody flowers, I expect, she muttered. She decided she was bored with the cupboards and wandered back into the living room clutching an air-fresh spray. Nothing like the scent of synthetic pine to cheer a room up, she always thought.

'I just wonder what I've got myself into,' Nancy was saying. 'I mean, maybe I came over like I wanted a freebie to Hong Kong – maybe when we're wed he'll resent it. Reckon I made all the running, you know.'

Donna sprayed the room with air freshener. 'He's all right, is Paddy Garvey,' she said. She looked round the living room in triumph. 'Look at that,' she said. 'Have you ever seen anything more hygienic?'

Donna was sleeping the sleep of the just when she

was woken by a row fit to wake the devil himself. Music. Laughter. Crashing glass and slamming doors. She leapt out of bed and grabbed her dressing gown.

She stormed downstairs. The party had come to her house. The floor was a mess of crushed crisps and cigarette ends. There were bottles on every surface and cans stuck down the sides of the chairs. There was Tony Wilton doing a bad Tom Jones impersonation. There was Paddy Garvey sprawled across her sofa with his feet up on the wall. And there was her Dave grinning stupidly and holding out a bowl of peanuts like he thought she was going to join in or something.

She grabbed it off him. 'Right, you bastards,' she roared. 'Piss off out.'

'Leave it out, Donna,' Tony Wilton said. He had a streamer round his neck, his shirt open to his waist and a can in each hand. 'I was building up to a crescendo.'

'Out!' Donna screamed.

Dave gave her his stupid little-boy grin that usually did the trick. 'Donna, I was going to phone but –'

'Get them out, Dave,' she yelled. She could feel the tears streaming down her face. She turned and fled, slamming the door after her.

Behind her, the music started up again.

Dave woke up feeling like a nuclear bomb was going off in his brain. Paddy was sprawled in the chair next to him, but Tony, being Tony, had crawled off home.

Donna came downstairs and started cleaning up. Loudly.

He'd barely got over that when Nancy arrived. She stormed in and helped Donna have a go at them. She was in full uniform, and in full flood she was quite something. Then she leaned over to Paddy and said in a low, dangerous voice, 'And you call yourself a Corporal?' She came round the front of the sofa and started to dump cans in a black bin-liner. 'You're nothing but a drunk. A wreck. A fool.' She leaned towards him. 'And a bully.'

Paddy surged up out of his seat. 'I am not a bully,' he roared. She was tall, but he towered over her and he was broad with it.

She wasn't intimidated though – quite something, Nancy Thorpe is when she gets going, Dave thought hazily. Could do a lot worse, Paddy my son. 'Oh no?' she yelled back. 'Ask Jimmy Monroe.' Paddy stared at her. 'Not the first time, is it?' she demanded. 'And if you think I'm lining up to be your next victim, Paddy Garvey, you can take your Special Licence and shove it where it'll do most good.' She started to walk off.

Paddy grabbed her arms. Bad move. She shrugged him off. 'What you going to do? Belt me?'

'If that's what it takes to make you listen,' Paddy said sullenly.

Nancy shoved him in the chest, hard. He stumbled back and fell into the sofa 'Oh shove it, Paddy,' she said. She went and talked quietly to Donna for a couple of minutes. Then she came back. She jabbed

31

her finger at Paddy. 'If I ever see you again, it'll be too soon.'

She left before Paddy could say a thing – which was probably just as well, in Dave's opinion, since anything he said was obviously going to be wrong.

They'd chosen the wrong day for the party. The day after the morning after the night before they had their last live firing exercise before they left for Hong Kong, and it was really not a good idea to be under the weather for it.

As far as Dave was concerned, the whole thing passed in a kind of blur – run here, keep your head down there. Stop, go – watch that bastard over there he's the *enemy*. The problem with live firing exercises was that they were just a bit too real – take your mind off it for a second and you might just find yourself walking into a live round.

Which, as it happened, is what Paddy nearly did – courtesy of Marilyn, of course. Who else?

It wasn't just a straightforward screw-up, though. There was something odd going on. It involved a lot of to-ing and fro-ing afterwards, a lot of talk between Paddy and Tony and Major Cochrane.

'Come on, Paddy,' Dave asked him in a rest period. 'I'm your mate – you can tell us.'

'Curiosity killed the cat, Dave,' Paddy said. He was definitely not his usual bright-eyed self. 'You'd do well to remember that.' He got up heavily and went off to talk to Cochrane. Again.

'Aye, Paddy,' Dave said to his retreating back. 'But at least the cat died happy.'

'There's a stain on the settee,' Donna wailed to Joy. She walked over to the sideboard. It was covered in full ashtrays and dead cans and bottles. 'And someone's spilled beer all over this.' She opened the top drawer – awkwardly, because she was wearing rubber gloves. 'Oh my God,' she said. Someone had upended a full foil tray of pilau rice into it.

The smell from it was disgusting, the more so because it mingled with the stink of stale ashtrays and old beer.

Joy came to inspect the damage. 'It's not as bad as you think,' she said, ever the optimist. 'Someone's just tipped it away – couldn't have been hungry.'

Sometimes optimism just wasn't what you wanted to hear. 'It's all gone solid on us,' Donna said. She looked at Joy hopelessly. 'What am I gonna do? I'm being marched out of here in two hours.'

'Right,' Joy said. Donna suddenly realized that there was nothing she liked better than something to organize or a problem to solve. 'We'll get them to postpone it till tomorrow, and you and I will roll our sleeves up and get this place sorted. I promise.'

That simple? Donna thought. She could have kissed Joy – she was even ready to forgive her for being married to Tony and his bloody Tom Jones impersonations.

Just then, Nancy turned up. She was as miserable as sin, but they'd got so used to it that Donna would have fainted dead away if Nancy had smiled at her. She went over and sat on the arm of the settee.

Joy went off into the kitchen making yet another

list, this time of cleaning products she hoped to find there. Donna didn't like to be a spoilsport, so she didn't bother to tell her that the only one of them she had any hope of finding was the vinegar.

'How's it going, hin?' she asked Nancy. No reply. 'Wedding nerves,' she said, patting the other woman gently on the arm.

Nancy sniffled. 'What wedding?' she said. 'I may be daft but I'm not certifiable.' She looked up at Donna. 'I can't marry Paddy – I don't even know who he is.'

Donna looked at her in bewilderment. 'Yes you do – he's the big soft sod with the blue eyes.' When that didn't raise a laugh, she pulled up a chair and said, 'Come on – tell Auntie Donna. Spit it out.'

'There was this kid in Paddy's class at school,' she said. 'Paddy and the others – they bullied him. And one day they chased him down on to the railway tracks and he fell under a train.' She stopped to wipe her nose. 'He died. Paddy chased him – he was the one that was closest to him.' She stopped again. 'Don't you see, Donna? He did it. My Paddy's a killer. And that new kid in the platoon – Monroe? – his brother was there. And now Paddy's taking it out on him – he's just a big bully, that's all.'

'Now I wouldn't say that – ' Donna started. Something in that story didn't sound right, but she couldn't put her finger on it. Before she had a chance to say any more, Joy came out of the kitchen.

She held out a couple of cans of cleaner. 'Is this all there is?' she said, like it was a major crime not to support the household products industry. She paused, realizing something was wrong. 'Is everything all right?'

Nancy got up. She grabbed a duster from Joy. 'Oh give us something to do, Joy – something to wring or punch or beat.' She went through into the kitchen.

'I'll lend you Dave if you like,' Donna called.

Nancy was waiting for Dave when he knocked off. She had her mind set on calling off the wedding, and since he was best man she wanted him to do the dirty work for her.

'Listen,' she said, 'I've heard all I want to hear, okay?'

They walked down the colonnade towards the women's accommodation block.

'Yeah,' Dave said. 'From every other prat you could round up. But not from Paddy.' He sighed heavily, wishing he'd managed to squirrel more out of Paddy earlier on. 'He deserves better than that, Nance.'

Nancy came to a halt. 'I know,' she said. 'But he was away training and I had a few things that needed sorting – '

'Well you get that all the time as an army wife,' Dave said. He was suddenly sick and tired of being on the wrong end of it, and of hearing Paddy – who was basically, in most people's opinion, a big soft-hearted lump even if he did look like a scrum half – getting slagged off. 'But if you call it off all the time . . .' he let his voice trail off. Nancy was bright – she could work it out.

'Look, I just need a bit more thinking time,' she said.

'Well, you haven't got it. The army clicks its fingers and we're off.' She was going to break Paddy's heart, Dave thought. It wasn't the kind of thing he usually thought about, but he knew it was true. The stupid thing was, she was going to break her own as well. 'But at least if you're together . . .' He stared at her. Her expression was unreadable. Well the least he could do was make it as hard as possible – that might just stop her doing it at all. 'The least you can do is tell the poor sod in person,' he said. He turned to go, but stopped and said over his shoulder, 'And don't go making out it's all his fault, neither.'

The Inspector was a round little man with glasses and a clipboard. Donna and Joy trailed him around as he went from room to room, looking in every cupboard and not only on every shelf but under it as well. Halfway through, Dave got back. He looked properly worried when Donna explained the system – and then properly amazed as he walked into the living-room.

Finally the Inspector pronounced himself satisfied and Donna was able to show him the door, which she'd been aching to do the moment he arrived. Everyone gathered on the step.

'Congratulations, Mrs Tucker,' he said. 'It's one of the best little houses I've seen. You must have been hard at it for days.'

Donna smiled. 'Oh no – you just take us as you find us.' She looked up at Dave. 'Don't you, pet?'

He grinned weakly.

When the Inspector left, Donna said, 'Right. Where'll we find that prat Paddy Garvey?'

'Aw, you aren't going to have a go at him as well, are you?' Dave said. 'Don't you think he's got enough on his plate what with Nancy?'

'Don't be daft, Dave Tucker,' Donna said. 'We're going to sort them out, that's what we're going to do.'

They found him alone in the bar, nursing a pint and looking as miserable as a man could look. Dave got a round in while Donna sat down with him. 'Now,' she said. 'I reckon you owe me one for the state of my flat, Paddy Garvey.'

'Oh aye,' he said wearily. 'I'm sorry about that, Donna.'

'And I suppose you're sorry for the state you've got poor Nancy in, as well?' she said.

Dave brought the drinks over. He put Donna's and Paddy's down in front of them. 'I'll just have a quick game of pool and then I'll be over,' he said. 'All right, pet?'

Donna smiled. 'What were you saying, Paddy?' There was no letting them off the hook. It wasn't good for them.

'She's upset because she found out I was involved in the death of a kid in the year below me at school,' Paddy said.

'I know,' Donna said. 'I want to hear your side of it.'

'It wasn't like she thinks,' Paddy said. He knocked back a third of a pint in a single swallow, then wiped away a foam moustache before he continued. 'We were chasing the kid – yeah, that's true. And I did bully him, like it said in the newspaper clipping that bastard Derry sent her.' He paused for another drink, and for a second Donna thought she'd lost him. 'But it was Derry that was at the front – Derry that hounded him on to the railway tracks. I saw what was going on – I saw he was on the track and that the train was coming. But he couldn't hear me. And afterwards, Derry scarpered. I stayed with the body, so when they found us it looked really bad for me.' He stopped again, but this time he didn't even bother with the drink. He just stared into space. 'I was only fifteen, and I wanted to tell someone – but every time I tried to say something, I just started crying.' He finished his pint.

Donna took a sip of her vodka and orange. 'Paddy Garvey, I was right first time.' He stared at her as if she were about to pass a death sentence. 'You are a great soft sod. Now just you go and find your Nancy, and tell her exactly what you just told me. It's what she's wanting to hear, you know.' She fumbled in her bag for a cigarette. Then she thought of something. 'Oh, and you can tell her I said she needs to be up first thing – we need to do something about that dress of hers.'

Paddy stood up. He swallowed. 'Okay,' he said. And then he grinned. 'Okay.'

'Are you ready, girls?' Nancy yelled. All three of them

38

were in adjoining cubicles in a posh frock shop in town – Nancy had finally despaired of finding anything she liked in a wedding shop.

'Ready,' Joy and Donna chorused.

'One. Two. Three,' Nancy shouted, and they all walked out at the same time.

They were wearing simple silk sheaths, slit to the thigh but high-necked – quite Chinese style, as Joy had pointed out, and just right for women about to go to Hong Kong.

Donna didn't know about that, but she could imagine Dave wanting to rip it off her slowly, and that was good enough for her.

The wedding went without a hitch. After all, as Donna said afterwards, everything that could go wrong already had.

'Oh, I don't know,' Dave confessed to Tony afterwards, 'There was a minute when I thought I'd left the ring at home – '

'Get off,' Tony said. 'I saw you check it three times, you pillock.'

Dave grinned. 'Well, I had to say I nearly lost it,' he conceded. 'I mean, I wouldn't want to ruin my reputation for messing things up, now would I?'

'You are a bloody nut case, you are,' Tony said.

'Oh aye,' Dave agreed. 'It's taken you this long to notice, then?' He stood up. 'I've just got one thing to do before the happy couple leave,' he said.

He found Marilyn sitting in a corner by himself.

The Major had decided he'd be better off out of it, and had found him a place on a drivers' course. Meanwhile, he had to rub along with the rest of them.

Dave popped a pint of lager down in front of him. 'There you go,' he said. 'Reckon I owe you that.'

Marilyn eyed him warily.

'No really,' Dave said. 'I mebbe overdid it a bit.' He took a pull on his own pint. 'Mind you, you're going to have to learn how to take a joke.'

'I suppose,' Marilyn said.

'And how to give as good as you get.' Dave drew patterns on the table with the wet ring his glass had left behind. 'You take our Paddy, now – he's really got it coming. And you won't get a better opportunity than this – he's completely off his guard.'

'I suppose so,' Marilyn said dubiously.

'Now a good practical joke takes planning,' Dave said. In fact, he'd already got the makings of it. He just needed a bit of brute force and ignorance to finish it off. 'But that's where this is your lucky day.' He paused. Marilyn still looked uncertain. 'Unless you haven't got the bottle for it?'

'No no,' the recruit said. 'I'm in . . .'

Paddy and Nancy left the reception as soon as they decently could. It was already dark, and there was a beautiful crescent moon in the sky.

Just enough light to follow them by, Dave whispered to Marilyn. Not enough so they'll spot us easily. They dashed from shadow to shadow as Paddy and Nancy walked towards the married quarters.

'Oh darlin',' Paddy said. 'I wish it were Hong Kong already, and this were a luxury hotel.' He had his arm round Nancy's shoulder, and she was holding him around the waist.

'Nah – too posh,' Nancy said.

'Or a grass hut in the Caribbean,' Paddy said.

'Bit rough.'

They were nearly at the married quarters. Dave was almost ready to explode with excitement. He and Marilyn found some cover in a doorway.

''Stead of a bloody married quarter in Ravens-bridge.'

'Ooh! said Goldilocks. It's just right.' Nancy pulled Paddy to a stop. They were just outside the married quarters they'd been allocated.

Dave nudged Marilyn. 'Any minute now,' he said.

Paddy pulled back from Nancy so he could look at her. 'My wife,' he said, in a voice touched with wonderment.

'My husband,' Nancy said. She giggled.

Paddy pulled her in for a kiss, but at the last minute he made it a quick peck on her forehead. 'Oh,' he sighed. 'I've been waiting for this all day.'

'Me too,' Nancy said shyly.

Paddy pulled her towards the doorway of the married quarter. He pulled out his key. Which was useless because Dave and Marilyn had bricked the doorway up.

'Oh no,' he said. He pounded his head slowly against the brickwork. He turned round and bellowed, 'Dave Tucker, I'm going to get you for this, you little shite!'

'See what I mean, Marilyn?' Dave hissed. 'It's just give and take.' He licked his lips and yelled, 'Take a cold shower instead, Paddy!'

Then he ran like hell.

Chapter 2

Hong Kong sweltered in the early morning heat, and the sunshine bouncing off the sea and the white concrete walls of the married quarters was bright enough to sear your eyeballs. Sweat trickled down Dave's back and made his hand slip in Donna's. He almost regretted arguing Donna out of a quiet afternoon by the pool, but he'd wanted to see a bit of the place before he went on duty.

Oh my God! what have we here, he thought as he caught sight of Paddy Garvey. The Corporal was wearing a red-and-white striped singlet and shorts, and he was brushing out a brightly coloured rug.

Dave raised his dark glasses for effect. 'What do you look like, you pillock?' he said as they walked past.

'Leave him alone,' Donna said, turning so they could continue the conversation. 'I think it's dead lovely.'

'Cleaning up for Nance,' Paddy yelled. He grinned and waved the brush in the air.

'Are you going to the airport to meet her?' Donna asked.

Paddy scowled. 'Not if Tony has his way – he won't let me have the time off – we've got our first duty with the new Lieutenant tomorrow.' He whacked the rug with the brush. 'But I can always hope.'

The lad had a lot to learn about married life, that was for sure, Dave thought. But that was okay, as long as he had Dave Tucker around to teach him.

'Leave it stinking – up to her knees in it when she walks in,' Dave advised. He grinned at Donna. 'Makes them feel needed –'

Donna rose to the bait beautifully. 'Southern Beirut, that's what I'd come home to.' She paused to consider. 'Only not so tidy.' Dave smiled, that naughty-boy grin that got her every time. She tugged him along the pavement. 'I know you, you bastard –' She thumped him gently on the belly with her white shoulder bag.

Oh aye, Dave thought. And I know you too. He wondered how much getting her to forget it would cost.

Donna was still half asleep when the phone went next morning. She threw the sheet off her and glared at the alarm clock. Dave was long gone and just as well – it was almost half past nine. She palmed the sleep out of her eyes with one hand while she picked up the receiver with the other.

'Donna?' said Joy's voice, made tinny by the phone line.

'What is it?' Donna asked, trying not to snap.

'It's Matthew, he won't stop crying,' Joy said. From the sound of her, he wasn't the only one. In the background, Donna could hear him yelling his little head off. Well, I'm sure I'm the right person to talk to, she thought. As far as she was concerned, babies were fine. She just couldn't eat a whole one. 'Can't you stick a dummy in his mouth or something, pet?'

She'd said the wrong thing. Get Joy in this mood, and everything was the wrong thing. 'Donna – ' Joy wailed.

'Oh come on, it can't be that bad – '

'It's not that, but my Tony had a right go at me this morning because I moved some papers, and – '

Moan, moan, moan. The sooner Joy learned to give as good as she got, the happier she'd be. 'Look pet, stick Matthew in his pushchair and we'll go and have a look round the market. Cheer you up a bit. Besides, I saw some tee-shirts yesterday and I want another look at them.'

'All right.' Joy sounded about as happy as if Donna had suggested she pull her own teeth out.

That was the trouble with some people. They were never happy.

Donna rolled over, pulled the sheet back up, and went back to sleep.

Number 1 Platoon stood at ease – which in Dave's opinion wasn't half easy enough – in the blistering heat of the Stanley Barracks parade ground, clothes neat, buttons, boots and belt buckles polished, and the blue-tipped hackle feathers in their berets at identical jaunty angles.

They were facing Pereira, the new Lieutenant.

45

Argie, Tony Wilton had told Dave. Argie but straight out of Sandhurst. More like straight out of the sand-pit, judging by the way he was carrying on, Dave thought. Still, he tried to look like he was paying attention, despite the headache he was getting from squinting into the sun. You had to humour him – let him have his fun while he could: he'd learn soon enough.

'It's about being a soldier,' Pereira said. Well, I'd never have guessed that, Dave thought. 'And that means hard work. Major Cochrane wants to command the top company, and I want to command the top platoon,' the Lieutenant continued. Here we go, Dave thought. It'll be the lean, mean fighting machine spiel next, I'll be bound. 'So we're going to be the leanest, meanest and keenest,' Pereira said, barely suppressing a grin.

Well, give the boy a banana, Dave thought. At least that was a variation on the old song. He grinned himself, hoping it didn't come over as sarcasm. Then he decided there was no need to worry: Pereira wouldn't recognize sarcasm if it jumped up and bit him on the bottom.

'Change of plan,' Pereira continued. 'Because we are being posted to the border in two weeks, I'm going to step up training. Number 2 Platoon have already done their speed march – '

Bloody hell, Dave thought. In this heat? The air was so humid it was fitter for swimming in than it was for breathing. Tony Wilton was standing next to

Pereira. Dave saw his mouth tighten almost imperceptibly. Go on, my son, Dave thought at him. Get us out of this.

'They were in the advance party, sir,' Tony said. If Dave hadn't known him so well, he might have missed the edge in his voice. 'They've already acclimatized.'

Pereira didn't miss a beat: ' – Nine-thirty tomorrow morning, it's our turn. We'll soon catch up – '

'We're on light duties, sir, what with the heat and all. I've booked the gym.'

'Oh come on, Sergeant Wilton,' as if he were trying to persuade a kid to eat its greens. 'Some of you have been here two weeks already.'

'Most of us haven't,' Tony persisted. Good man, Dave thought. 'And I'm battalion orderly sergeant until nine tomorrow morning.'

'We're soldiers, Sergeant Wilton. Not Girl Guides – ' Bloody cheek, Dave thought. 'Back here at two and we'll have a chat about the march.'

Rather you than me, Dave thought.

'Carry on, Sergeant Wilton,' Pereira said. He crossed to the side of the parade ground.

''Toon!' Tony screamed. Pereira reached his position. ''Toon *'shun!*.'

Platoon Number 1 came to attention with a single crash of stamping feet. Tony saluted, still staring straight at the platoon. Pereira returned the salute, then turned and left.

'Okay,' Tony said. 'You heard Mr Pereira.' He glared at the platoon as if it were their fault, but Dave could hear the annoyance he couldn't quite hide. 'Fall out!'

The platoon stamped, turned and stamped again, all as one. Then they marched off, but within a few paces they were simply walking.

Dave caught Midnight up. 'Argentinian,' he said without trying to disguise his disgust. 'Sent to balls up the British army from the inside.'

'It's his Latin blood, isn't it?' Midnight said. He pouted and said in a falsetto, 'Perfume behind his ears.'

Wet behind the ears, you mean, Dave thought. But he didn't say it. He had a horrible feeling things were going to get much worse before they got better.

Stanley market was a riot of colours so loud they fairly shouted at you, and full of people shouting so loudly you couldn't understand a thing they were saying. And it smelled. Donna could pick out coconut and pineapple, but there were other scents she couldn't put a name to.

Not that she cared. Matthew hadn't stopped yelling his head off since they left the married quarters, and Joy hadn't been much better.

Bloody market was a rip off too. Donna fingered a cobalt blue tee-shirt.

Matthew wailed. 'It's no good, Donna,' Joy said. 'I'm going to have to take him home – give that doctor another ring.'

Donna glanced at Joy, then turned back to the stall. 'How much is this one?' she asked round a mouthful of gum.

'Twenty dollar,' said the Chinese stallholder, holding up two fingers.

'Twenty dollars?' Donna exclaimed. 'Harraway – '

'Donna, that's only one pound fifty – '

Oh thank you very much, Joy, Donna thought. 'Shh,' she said.

Just then, a small Chinese woman came up to Joy. She tried to push a figurine – a Buddha, would that be? Donna was too interested in the tee-shirt to take much notice – into Joy's hand.

'No thank you, I'm not interested,' she said firmly, just as Donna offered the Chinese boy fifteen dollars for the tee-shirt.

After all, everyone knew you were supposed to haggle in these foreign markets.

The boy held up his fingers again. 'Twenty dollar.'

'Eighteen.'

'Twenty.'

Donna scowled and started fumbling in her purse. Two fingers? She'd give him two fingers all right.

'He's ever so poorly,' Joy said.

Donna glanced at her. 'Shame,' she said, chewing furiously. She pulled out a twenty-dollar bill and pushed it at the stallholder. 'There you are then,' she said. 'And it's not bloody worth it.' She stuffed her purse back in her shoulder-bag. 'Dump him on your amah,' she said. Best thing for him – get him used to going to school. At least that was what her mam used to say when she dumped Donna on Auntie Vi.

'She doesn't know what she's doing.' Joy sounded affronted. No pleasing some people, Donna thought.

'Anyway, he's got these blisters that have come up right on his groin – ' How lovely, Donna thought, as she shoved the tee-shirt into her shopping bag. Tight so-and-so hadn't even put it in a paper bag.

They set off through the market. 'Anyway,' Joy said after a bit. 'I've got stuff to get for Tony's birthday. Got Nancy coming round – '

'Dave never said,' Donna exclaimed. 'We were going to take her down to that steak house.' Joy stared at her. She didn't seem very happy, Donna thought, but that was probably worrying about the bairn. Well, a good night out would fix that, quick enough. 'What time do you want us?' she asked.

Before Joy could answer, she spotted a stall selling silk scarves and darted off to look at them.

You could have cut the atmosphere in the reception of the guard-house with a knife. Paddy was getting his knickers in a twist because Tony wouldn't let him have time off to meet Nancy from her flight, but Tony wasn't shifting an inch.

Dave listened as he swept the store-room.

'Come on, Sarge,' Paddy said. 'She'll be here in three-quarters of an hour.'

Dave grinned. Fat chance, not with Tony still in a snit over the fast one old Argie-bargy had pulled on them. And who could blame him? He pushed the broom closer to the reception, so he could hear better.

Tony faced the pinboard, pointedly reading a memo. If his back could have talked it would have been swearing at Paddy like an RSM. 'Paddy,' he said. 'I'm twenty-seven, tomorrow. Joy's been nagging me all day. It's thirty-two degrees in the shade. Matthew's sick. Don't drive me mad. All right?' By the time he finished, he was shouting.

Dave moved into the reception. 'It's the humidity,' he said. Anything to lighten the atmosphere. 'We could all drop dead at any minute.' Tony and Paddy stared at him with disbelief written all over their faces. 'It's true,' he said, miffed. 'Happened once.' He started to tell the story, only to find Paddy joining in with him. 'A bloke I know went to Butlin's – ' Tony turned his back. 'Dropped dead. Heatstroke.'

They didn't believe him. They never did. He was used to it. But when they were all dead, he'd have the last laugh –

Tony turned, stood to attention and saluted. Pereira appeared in the doorway. Paddy got up. Dave leaned the brush against Paddy's desk and stood up straight.

'So,' Tony said, as if it were a natural follow-on to what they had been talking about, 'Keep an eye open for drunks. And no letting hawkers through in the morning. This Duty is all about camp security. It matters. Got me?'

'Looking very good, Sergeant. Thank you,' Pereira said.

'I'll just check the side gate, sir.'

The two men saluted, and Tony left.

'I'll be in the mess, Corporal,' Pereira said. He turned to go.

Paddy hesitated for a second. 'Oh sir,' he said. He dashed round the desk in time to stop Pereira leaving.

Don't do this, Paddy, Dave thought. Breaking the chain of command by going over Tony's head could only lead to disaster.

'My wife's just arriving in from the UK on tonight's flight. I thought . . . if there were any chance . . .'

Pereira smiled sympathetically. 'Bit late to ask, isn't it?'

You don't know the half of it, Dave thought.

'Well, we've got guard duty tonight, and then we're away on the march tomorrow, sir.'

'Not as if we had any warning, sir,' Dave pitched in. You had to admire Paddy's gall, and besides Tony I'm-a-Sergeant-now could do with teaching a bit of a lesson.

'Only been married a month, sir,' Paddy wheedled.

'Garvey, right?' Pereira asked. He smiled conspiratorially. 'Go on then. But make it bloody quick.'

Paddy almost ran out of the guard-house. He paused to give Dave a thumbs-up from behind Pereira's back.

The lieutenant lit up a cigarette. 'Okay?' he asked Dave.

'I am, sir,' Dave said as he went back to his sweeping up.

Nothing as easy as twisting a baby officer round your little finger, he thought. Especially if they wanted you to like them.

It ended in tears, of course, just like Dave knew it

would. The trouble started a bit later, when Tony came back. Dave was on the desk, signing out some lucky so-and-so from Number 2 Platoon who was going out for the evening. Behind him, Midnight stood chewing a wad of gum and generally being useless.

Tony came in through the door, calling for Paddy. He had his swagger stick tucked under his arm and that grin on his face that meant he'd thought of some particularly useless way for the platoon to spend the afternoon.

That changed the minute he saw Lieutenant Pereira lounging against the wall with a cigarette in one hand and that let's-all-be-best-mates grin on his face.

'I gave him permission to meet his wife,' Pereira said.

Dave found something fascinating to read in the log-book.

Tony's jaw worked. 'What?' he said. He looked away. 'Shit!' The word exploded out of him. He took a deep breath. 'At this time of night, sir? Have you seen the traffic? He's guard commander, sir.'

'Never a problem in the Girl Guides,' Midnight said in a squeaky voice.

Never did know when to keep shtum, didn't Midnight, Dave thought. He stared out the door and waited for the explosion.

Tony didn't disappoint him. He jabbed his swagger stick in Midnight's direction. 'Shut it Rawlings!' he screamed. 'And take that gum out of your mouth before I knock it out.' He glared at Midnight and lowered the stick very slowly.

53

A little ball of gum pinged into the metal waste-paper basket.

Without taking his eyes off Midnight, Tony said, 'All right, sir. I'll nip over to the Corporals' Mess and try and sort something out.' His tone was expressionless. 'Tucker, you keep an eye on things.'

Tony left. Pereira put his cigarette in his mouth and flicked his Bic lighter over and over again without managing to get a light.

'Not to worry, sir,' Dave said.

Midnight stuffed another stick of gum in his mouth.

Come on, Tone, Dave thought as he leaned out of the guard-house window. Hurry up and get us sorted out. But it was impossible to worry too much. Dusk had fallen suddenly, and a cool sea-breeze had begun to blow in. The indigo sky was pierced by stars and, Dave reckoned, you could get to like Hong Kong —

If you didn't know the shit was about to hit the fan any second.

A figure walked across the yard. In the darkness it was impossible to see who it was, but the shape was about right for Tony.

The person came into the light of the porch just as he said, 'Corporal, I'm off to see if some alcohol will lower my body —' Shit, Dave thought. Cochrane. The major took the porch steps two at a time, and came up to Dave. 'What the hell is going on here?' he demanded.

Dave hesitated, unsure what he could say without

landing someone in it. Cochrane almost quivered with indignation as he turned away. Dave backed over to the desk, where he wouldn't seem to be listening in, but from where he could still get a good view of the fireworks.

Pereira met him at the door. 'Major Bob,' he said. Dave couldn't see his face, but he could imagine the little-boy lost grin. It might have worked well enough when he was a kid, but to a bastard like Cochrane it would just be an invitation to give him a kicking.

'Where's the guard commander?' Cochrane demanded.

'Sergeant Wilton's just getting him, sir,' Pereira said. It was true as far as it went, Dave supposed. But of course the Lieutenant couldn't leave it there. 'I gave him a bit of time off – '

There was a pause. Dave winced. It was like Pereira had just pulled the pin from a grenade.

'Lieutenant Pereira, a word – ' Cochrane said, in a voice like a controlled explosion.

The two officers started down the porch steps. Damn, Dave thought. But just then Tony turned up with Davies, a corporal from Number 3 Platoon.

'Oh, this is Corporal Garvey, is it?' Cochrane said. 'My how you've changed, Grandmama.' He kept his gaze on Pereira the whole time.

Sarky git, Dave thought.

The phone shrilled.

'Get that phone, Tucker,' Cochrane snapped. Dave picked up the phone. It was Joy, and she was obviously upset, but Dave could hardly hear her because of Cochrane's shouting. 'Orderly! Sergeant!' he screamed. Joy'll hear, Dave thought. Any minute now she'll ask why Tony's in trouble. 'As such you have direct responsibility for NCOs and for the security of this camp – '

Dave murmured something comforting at Joy, but his heart wasn't in it.

Not with Cochrane yelling his head off outside. 'If you can't hack the third stripe, just let me know, Sergeant.' Tony had gone pale. He swallowed.

'Are you going to put Tony on?' Joy asked.

Dave muttered a 'yes' down the phone at her. 'It's for you, Sergeant,' he said. 'Your wife.'

Cochrane glared at Tony for another second or two. Then he turned to Pereira, and Tony was able to come inside. Dave handed him the phone.

Outside he heard Cochrane say, 'I'm back at ten. The Mess. And get a grip of this guard. They're walking all over you.' He stalked off.

Well, only because you're such a doormat, Dave thought. Mind you, he couldn't help feeling a bit sorry for the bloke – he looked like a kid who'd just gone ten rounds with the headmaster and lost.

Dave lounged in the doorway between the reception and the back room – he wanted to see what happened, but he also wanted to be able to duck out if he had to.

Tony wasn't having such a good time either. 'No,' he said down the phone. 'Of course I do,' he whispered.

Ah, thought Dave. The old 'You don't love me any

more' routine. Always a good one to pull out when the poor bugger concerned was with his mates. Donna had taught him that, long ago.

Pereira walked in and planted himself by the desk. Tony glanced up. 'I have to go,' he muttered and put the phone down quickly.

'Couldn't you have switched his duties so he could meet his wife?' Pereira asked gently.

Time to go, Dave thought, at least if I wanted to be discreet. But he'd never thought discretion was the better part of valour, so he stayed where he was.

'He'd have had tomorrow with her, sir,' Tony said, equally gently. Give 'im one for us, Dave thought. Tony went on, 'But then you dreamed up the speed march without telling me. We do have families, sir. We do have social lives.'

Pereira had the good grace to look embarrassed. Before he could say anything, Tony turned away.

Grenade time, Dave thought. One, two –

'Right,' Tony yelled, 'This is Number 1 Platoon. We will not backslide into a total bloody shambles – not while I'm in charge. Got it?'

Got it, Dave thought.

Chapter 3

The parade ground blistered in the morning heat. It was still only nine-thirty. Dave stood next to Midnight, forcing down more of the water in his canteen. It was warm and metallic-tasting, and it caught at the back of his throat. Sweat stung his eyes. He swiped at it, and his hand came away black from the stripes of camo smeared across his face.

There was a backpack stuffed with sandbags at his feet. From here, things could only get worse.

'Sergeant Wilton,' Pereira shouted from the front of the crowd. 'Have you checked the water bottles? I want them empty.' Dave knew the Lieutenant was talking as much to the men as to Tony. 'And you're all carrying another two full bottles each. It's not pleasant, but it's better than heatstroke.'

Aye, thought Dave. And so is not going on this march at all until we're used to the place.

'You heard the gentleman, Tucker,' Tony said from behind him.

Damn, Dave thought. He stared down at his canteen in mock surprise that there was anything left in it.

Pereira hooked a spring balance on to one of the backpacks. 'Thirty-five pounds minimum,' he said.

We'll soon see about that, Dave thought. Pereira stared straight at him. 'Oh, and I'll weigh them again at the other end.' He let the pack drop. 'Just in case any bright sparks manage to lose any bits and pieces on the way.'

Now why's he looking at me like that, Dave thought. Would I do such a thing? Would I dream of it?

Next to him, Paddy Garvey was helping Midnight to settle his pack on his shoulders. 'Oh what a clever little officer we are,' Midnight murmured.

Pereira glared at him.

'We were just saying, sir,' Paddy said quickly, 'That it's Sergeant Wilton's birthday.' He tugged savagely on Midnight's shoulder strap.

'The less you have to say for yourself after last night's bloody fiasco, the better,' Tony said.

'Twenty-one again, Sergeant Wilton?' Pereira asked. Still wants us to like him, Dave thought as he swigged back the last of his water. Some people never learn.

'It's been a long time since I was twenty-one, Mr Pereira,' Tony said. He stalked off.

You hardly needed the heat and humidity, Dave thought. Just put Pereira and Tony in one room and you got the worst atmosphere you could imagine.

The walls of the married quarters were paper thin. Typical bloody army, Donna thought. Joy was shouting at her amah again. It was the third time she'd woken Donna up the same way.

'Mela,' she shouted. 'Mela, just come out of there.'

Donna rolled over in bed. She would have put the pillow over her head to block out the sound, but it was just too hot.

'Mela, please – '

Bloody hell, Donna thought. She rolled back over, sat up and grabbed her dressing-gown. Time for a cuppa, she thought, as she shambled towards the kitchen. But just because she'd got up, she didn't have to go next door to Joy.

Rotting cabbage, Dave thought. That was what he could smell: a sickly sweet odour that caught the back of his throat and made his stomach churn.

The stink had hit him when he first got out on the mountainside. He'd thought they were just walking by a stagnant pool, but the smell had stayed with him all the time they were marching round the mountain. The worst of it was, it changed from moment to moment. It was always disgusting, but it was never the same long enough for him to get used to it.

All he could do was put one foot in front of the other, and try to ignore the stench and the weight of Pereira's damned sandbags hauling at his shoulders and the slap, slap, slap of the rifle hanging against his hip, and pretend that sooner or later the mountain would come to an end.

They'd only been going two hours.

At least Pereira wasn't setting too fast a pace.

'Right,' he yelled. 'Two miles to the safety vehicle. Fresh water and a five-minute break – '

'Five whole minutes, Midnight,' Dave hissed.

'Long enough to practise my Argentinian,' Midnight muttered back.

'Spanish, Rawlings,' Pereira said, from behind Dave. Here we go, Dave thought — ickle baby officer wants to be one of the boys again.

Well, what the hell? It would end in tears, but it might be fun while it lasted.

He glanced back. The sweat had turned Pereira's shirt dark, and reduced the black camo to a fine grey film; but he hefted his weapon easily enough, and by the grin on his face he might have been out for a walk in the garden.

'I said you wasn't an Argie, sir,' Midnight said. He sounded pleased.

'No, they speak Spanish,' Pereira said.

'Say something then, sir,' Dave said.

'Argentina five,' Pereira said in a thick Spanish accent. 'England nil.'

He stopped walking, so the rest of the line went past him.

'Cheeky bastard!' Midnight said.

Dave grinned. Pereira laughed, somewhere behind him. There were worse things than wanting to be one of the lads, of course, Dave thought.

A couple of minutes later, Tony yelled, 'Get a move on you lazy bastards!' in that tone he kept for when he was pissed off about something at home.

So that meant Pereira had managed to get up his nose again.

Well, Dave thought, you win some and lose some. He took another swig out of his water bottle.

* * *

Five-minute break, Pereira had said. He hadn't bothered to tell them he was going to make them double their pace afterwards. Dave's feet pounded against the yellow earth of the jungle trail.

'Left, left, left,' yelled Tony – or perhaps it was Pereira – from the front.

The pace picked up. The trail led close to a stream, and the air was thick with the smell of rotting fruit. Mosquitoes buzzed round Dave's face, but he couldn't spare the time even to flap them away.

In the stream, a lump of something – a log, a tangled mass of vegetation, maybe even a dead animal, Dave was past it too fast to say – bumped against the bank in the slow current.

The path took a sharp turn uphill. Nestled against the side of the mountain there was a small bamboo hut. From inside it there came the soft glow of many candles, and a blue swirl of incense-laden smoke. Dave slowed his pace and let others pass him. He wanted to get a good look at this. Broaden his horizons, like. No point coming all this way round the world and not learning a bit.

And if it gave him a chance to catch his breath, well, what could it hurt? Old Argie-bargy would never even notice. Dave stopped completely.

He glanced up the trail. He hadn't been noticed – the others were away up the mountainside. All except Midnight, who came to a halt next to him. Together, they looked into the hut.

Inside, there was a young Chinese man, with one of the wide-brimmed hats they wore slung across his back. He was standing in front of a table – an altar, Dave supposed – on which there was a statue, and a mass of candles and burning incense. There were dozens of little pictures and trinkets. The man said something in Chinese, then backed away from the table. Dave saw that there was a bowl on a tripod in front of the altar. The man knelt and bowed, over and over again.

Midnight glanced anxiously down the trail at the others' backs, which were rapidly disappearing among the green dappled shadows.

'We'd better catch them up,' he said. He jerked his thumb at the shrine. 'That is, if you've finished sight-seeing.'

Dave thought about it for all of two seconds. Beyond the shrine, the stream opened out into a shallow pool. They'd get a bollocking, for sure: but they'd get one anyway.

He nodded towards the pool. 'Might as well be hung for a swim as a skive,' he said.

Midnight grinned and followed Dave towards the pool. He reached into his top pocket and pulled out a forbidden packet of chewing gum. He took a piece, then thumbed the next one out and offered it to Dave, who took it. While he was still unwrapping it, Midnight broke into a trot.

'Last one in's an Argie bastard,' he yelled over his shoulder.

'Hurry up, you Argie bastard,' Midnight yelled. 'It's magic.'

Dave was crawling along a tree that had grown out across the pool. The bark had the colour and texture of old rope, and it was dappled with leaf shadows. Below him, Midnight was standing knee deep in the brown water. He'd stripped to his waist, and drops of moisture clung to his dark skin. He was still wearing his trousers, and the water plastered the heavy material to his body, making Dave glad he'd stripped to his underpants.

Dave paused. He put his hand down carefully – he wasn't afraid of heights, but the ground below was covered with spiny, spiteful-looking plants – and said, 'Maradona's not going to be too happy.'

'Mr Paella?' Midnight said. He grabbed his nipples and gave them a good shake. 'Tough titty.'

What the hell, Dave thought. It was too late to worry about it now. He clambered carefully to his feet, and stood swaying on the branch. Sunlight glinted on the water, and ripples shattered the reflections of the trees that surrounded the pool.

It would be perfect, ice cold and well worth the bollocking they were going to get. Dave picked his spot, raised his arms above his head, tensed his body and prepared to leap in –

'Stand still!' Midnight yelled. He looked panic-stricken.

Dave froze. Christ, he thought, what is it? Scorpion, maybe? Did they get scorpions here? Or a spider? You got those everywhere . . . but Midnight was pointing past his head, to a clump of foliage.

'Don't . . . move,' he said.

64

Dave rolled his eyes round without moving his head, trying to see whatever it was . . . Snake, that was it. He was suddenly sure. A great green and yellow snake, with fangs dripping poison. He could hear the leaves rustling, coming closer and closer –

He couldn't stand it. 'What is it?' he asked, not wanting to hear the answer.

Midnight whipped his hands up in front of his face. He made a square of his thumbs and fingers, and peered through them as if they were a camera view-finder. 'I want to remember you just the way you are,' he said, falsetto.

It took Dave a full half-second to catch on. Then he bellowed Tarzan-style, and leapt feet first into the pool. He landed with an almighty splash and felt his feet sink into the silt. Midnight whacked the water with his hand. Right, you bugger, Dave thought. This is war. He grabbed Midnight's head and ducked him. He stood up, wiping the water out of his eyes. When he could see again, Midnight had vanished.

He looked around. Maybe he'd done a runner and was, even now, flogging Dave's gear off to the young monk. Or –

Something grabbed Dave's legs. Before he could re-act, he found himself being lifted up. He looked down. Midnight's head broke the water, and Dave realized he was now sitting on the other man's shoulders. He whooped with glee, and let himself fall backwards into the water. Midnight came after him. Dave turned and flailed water at him, and for a while they messed around like a couple of kids at the sea-side.

Eventually, Midnight started to climb out. Dave charged at him from behind and leapt on his back. Midnight staggered.

'Yeeharr!' Dave screamed. He flailed the air with his arm, as if waving a stetson around.

'Geddoffa me, you nut case,' Midnight roared. He twisted his torso so that Dave had to cling on. 'Get out of it,' Midnight said.

'Yes. You better bloody well had,' said Tony's voice from somewhere off to the side.

Dave looked round. Tony was standing in the shade of the tree he had jumped from. He was pale with anger. Paddy was just behind him. He had a bit of cloth tied round his head, Rambo-style. He had that blank look on him that meant he was as furious as it was possible for him to be.

A muscle jumped in Tony's cheek. 'Get out, get dressed and get a fucking move on,' he said quietly.

Dave would have preferred it if he'd screamed. 'Yes, Sarge,' he muttered. Midnight was already half-way out of the water. Dave followed him.

Tony jerked the yellow tip of his rifle barrel at the clothes, which they had left piled up near the tree. 'Get them on,' he said.

Dave shivered, suddenly chilled by the water drying on his skin. 'Have a heart, Sarge,' he said. 'We're all wet.'

'You are wet all right,' Tony snarled. 'But you'll soon warm up with the roasting Pereira's going to give you.' He paused for breath. His moustache wiggled. Somewhere in the trees, a parakeet squawked.

'Now get your clothes on, Fusilier. Or do I have to dress you myself?'

Dave turned away, making a sour face as soon as he was sure Tony couldn't see him, and picked up his combat trousers.

'Get a move on,' Tony said; and then, as soon as they were dressed: 'Right. On the double. Set the pace, Corporal.'

Paddy jogged off in the direction of the temple. Dave followed, with Midnight right behind him. As soon as they got to the path, Paddy speeded up. Dave's wet trousers clung to his legs, and his boots were sodden with water, so that he felt as if he were running with ten-pound weights tied to his ankles.

The path stretched out before him, lined on either side by a tangle of bushes and trees. Soon it was sweat rather than river water that sheened his face. He concentrated on Paddy's back, on the camouflage pattern on his jacket that moved with every pace he took.

The trees opened out to cleared fields, where peasants with home-made tools hoed the rows of whatever it was they were growing. They stared at Dave and the others. A little girl giggled and said something behind her hand to one of the older women.

Then they were past her, and running through a village of surprisingly neat white cottages. A deep black shadow beckoned, cool as water, where the eaves of one of the buildings almost touched the next. Dave looked at it longingly.

'Get a move on, Tucker!' Tony screamed. An old

man leaned on his spade and regarded them unblinkingly. 'With your luck this'll turn out to be a Triad stronghold.'

Oh aye, Dave thought. And there's reds under the beds and the mafia in the khazi. But he picked up speed. Better show willing.

The rest of the platoon were waiting for them round the next bend. They were sitting around in the shade of a broad-leafed tree, in a bit of meadow whose grass was studded with large urns.

'Run, you useless bastards!' Tony screamed. 'Run!'

Pereira came up to meet them. Paddy got to him first.

'They were right back, sir,' he said as he went past the officer.

Dave held his breath, but Paddy didn't say anything about the swimming. A good mate, Paddy. Dave could only hope Tony was the same.

Pereira looked at his watch just as Dave got to him. 'Yes, well, we don't stand a bloody chance now, do we?' He almost spat the words at Dave.

Paddy perched on one of the urns. Immediately an old man, who could have been the twin of the one in the village, came up and started whacking at him with his bamboo rake. Paddy leapt up, raising his arms to defend himself.

'Keep your hair on,' he said. He went over to Pereira.

Here we go, Dave thought. If he comes out with it and asks Paddy what we were doing –

But Pereira only said mildly 'You were probably

68

sitting on his grandmother.' He had the map under his arm. Now he unfolded it as he walked towards the tree where Dave, Midnight and most of the other men were waiting. He raised his eyebrows at Tony. When the Sergeant reached him, he finished flapping open the map and said, 'Right, let's see if we can make up for some of this lost time.' He pointed at something on the map.

'What?' Tony said. He sounded incredulous. Whatever it was, Dave thought, it was bad. 'Over the mountain? you must be joking, sir.' Pereira just stared at him. Wrong again, Tucker, Dave thought to himself. It isn't bad. It's insane. Tony glanced wildly around as if seeking inspiration. 'What about the back-up vehicle?' he said at last.

'We'll radio them,' Pereira said. He walked off before Tony could argue with him. 'Come on, lads,' he said to the platoon at large. 'On your feet.' He clapped a couple of times. 'Let's go. Let's go.'

As the men were getting to their feet, Tony gestured to Pereira. 'Sir?' he said. 'Sir, can I have a word?' His voice had gone high and tight, the way it always did when he had something embarrassing to say. He went on without meeting Pereira's eyes. 'We're never going to make up the time now, sir, so what's the rush?'

Pereira glared at him, and Dave was suddenly very glad he wasn't the one wearing the three stripes. The Lieutenant leaned very close to Tony, but he said in a voice loud enough for everyone to hear, 'Because I say so, Sergeant Wilton.' He went over to the tree

Midnight was leaning against. 'And because although we've been stuffed I would like us to put in a half decent time.' He glared at Midnight, who just looked at him blankly and rubbed the back of his neck with one enormous hand.

Dave wandered towards him, but that took him past Paddy and Tony, who were talking.

'I'm going to be late for my poxy dinner now,' Tony muttered.

That'll please Joy, Dave thought. He was going to say something, but he thought better of it. As he went past, Tony shoved his face up close to him. 'All thanks to you, you useless bastard,' he snarled.

He pushed between Dave and Paddy. 'Well, I haven't cancelled the steakhouse yet,' Dave said to his retreating back. Tony didn't say anything, but his shoulders braced just a bit, so Dave knew he'd heard. Can't take a joke, that's his trouble, Dave thought. He turned back to Paddy. 'Just in case,' he explained.

Paddy had a mouthful of water. He spat it out all over Dave, who could only stand there dripping till the order came to march out.

Pereira set a punishing pace, straight up the pitch of the mountain, through the thickest part of the jungle. The trees arched overhead into a vast green canopy, but the shade gave no relief from the heat. Water dripped from the leaves, and the air was thick with a swampy, rotting-vegetable smell. Birds shrieked and screamed and flew up in a welter of bright plumage in protest at the soldiers' approach. Foliage slapped at Dave's face and the ground underfoot was treacherous with mulch and knotted roots.

'Get a move on,' Tony Wilton yelled from somewhere up ahead, and Paddy ran a little faster.

Dave didn't know how long they had been running, or how far they had come. There was only the pounding of his feet against the earth that sent his pack jolting against his spine, and the camouflaged back of the man in front of him, hard to see in the patched light and shadow beneath the trees. He turned back to Midnight, ready to make a crack about what the Argentinians usually did in the jungle, but the man was running along, his gaze fixed on the ground as he tried to avoid catching his feet on a root or fallen branch.

Then again, he was probably worried about the what-for they were going to get when they got back to camp. Hadn't been around long enough to know that there wasn't much old Maradona could do to them. At least, Dave reckoned there wasn't.

He realized he'd been hearing the sound of running water for some time. The way was suddenly blocked by a limestone boulder at least twice as tall as Dave. Beyond it, a ribbon of blue sky arched across a torrent of water that broke over a jumble of rocks into a handful of little cataracts.

'Come on, you lot, don't break the pace,' Paddy yelled. He didn't stop to watch them, but scrambled up the crag.

Dave started up the rock. It was an easy enough climb, with plenty of handholds in the jointed, weathered rock. Foot up, hand, foot – and then he was clambering on to the top of the boulder. He glanced back. Midnight was making heavy going of it, but there was nothing Dave could do because Paddy was screaming at him to get a move on. He trotted across the boulder, hopped across to the next rock and the next, trying not to think about how slick with water the stone was, trying not to be distracted by the magnificent view.

Pay good money to get brought up here, tourists would, he thought, as he risked a quick scan down the river, where the water chattered against the rocks below them.

Then they were across, and back into the jungle; but not for long: the trees once again gave way to a river. This time it was broader and shallower, with a jumble of rocks strewn across it. Dave squinted into the sun, and followed the man ahead of him across.

'I've a wife to get home to, Rawlings,' Paddy shouted.

Dave looked back. Midnight was labouring to get across the stepping stones, and he was holding back the men behind him.

Heatstroke, Dave thought. 'Here,' he said. He held his water canteen out, without stopping still. 'Have a swig of this.'

Midnight took the canteen. He stared at it as if he couldn't work out what it was for. His face was shiny with sweat, and his expression was glazed.

'Nah,' he said after a bit.

Dave took the canteen back and clipped it to his belt. Up ahead, Paddy had stopped at the edge of the river and was screaming at people to get a move on.

Dave was almost up to him when he realized that Midnight had stopped. Despite Paddy's disapproving glare, he went over to a rock by the river and laid his gun down. Midnight stumbled over to him. He almost collapsed against the stone, but managed to turn and sit down at the last minute.

Christ, Dave thought. It wasn't just heatstroke, not by a long way. 'Give us your pack, Midnight,' he said, and started to yank on the webbing at Midnight's waist.

Paddy came up behind them. 'What are you two playing at?' he demanded.

Dave scowled. 'Doctors and nurses – what does it look like?' he said, not bothering to keep the sarcasm out of his voice. If Paddy couldn't see that Midnight was in trouble, he ought to give back both stripes as soon as they hit camp.

But Paddy seemed to realize something was wrong. 'You all right, mate?' he asked without a trace of anger.

'I need . . .' Midnight started. 'I need to sit here.'

Dave took Midnight's face in both hands and made the man look at him. 'Look, just one more hill, man, hey?' he said.

The water, he thought, remembering the pool where they had swum. Dark brown, stagnant water. There could have been anything in it – a dead pig, say, or human turds. He hadn't thought of it at the time, but he should have. And now Midnight was paying for it.

Paddy touched Midnight's forehead, then laid his hand right across it. 'He's burning up.'

Midnight slumped forwards, as if his neck couldn't support the weight of his head.

Paddy looked round, and if Dave hadn't known him better he would have sworn the Corporal was on the edge of panic.

'You stick here, Dave,' he said. He patted Midnight on the shoulder 'Sit tight, Midnight. I'll be back,' he said, as he got up and ran full tilt up the hillside, pushing past the last few squaddies.

All Dave could do was cradle Midnight's burning head in his arms as he watched the Corporal go.

Donna juggled the things she was carrying – a present for Tony and a bottle of fizzy wine – so she could ring Joy's doorbell. Music blared out from inside, and she could hear Nancy Garvey laughing, too.

Get a move on, she thought at the door; and at that moment, Joy opened it. She smiled. Well, that's a relief, pet, Donna thought. For a while she had wondered if Joy really wanted her to come.

'Come on in,' Joy said. She looked tired, but closer to happy than Donna had seen her in a long time.

'You look happy,' she said as she followed Joy into the kitchen.

'Well, I had a good talk to Mrs Fortune –' the Colonel's wife, Donna thought that explained a lot.

'Oh, it was you she was here to see, was it?' Donna asked. 'I bumped into her on my way out –'

'She's really nice,' Joy said. Then again, Joy thought everyone was really nice.

Nancy walked into the kitchen. 'Table's done,' she said. 'Got the wineglasses?'

'I was just saying, I bumped into Mrs Fortune earlier on,' Donna said as Joy got the glasses out. 'I was waiting for the lift, and I said to her, "they want to sort the bloody lift out, not be painting the kerbstones white like the Colonel wants. Sitting around all day on his fat arse . . ."'

'Donna!' That was Joy. Nancy giggled. They all started through into the front room, Nancy and Donna carrying wine glasses, Joy following with a small vase of flowers.

'So she just looks at me, and I say, "How much do you think the Colonel gets?" And she never said nothing. And I'm thinking, "Who is this chick? I haven't seen her around." So I say, "Who are you married to, anyway?"'

'Donna!' Joy exclaimed again.

'So she looks me straight in the eye and says, "Oh, I'm married to the fat-arsed bastard with the thing about kerbstones . . ."' Donna slammed the wineglasses down on the table and collapsed on to the dining chair, giggling hysterically.

Joy put the vase down in the precise centre of the table. 'Still, she's doing her best,' she said. She tweaked the flowers. 'And it's a bit different from Fleet Street.'

'Oh aye,' Donna said. She suddenly noticed that Joy's amah was sitting on the sofa, quietly fanning baby Matthew who was gurgling contentedly to himself. That made a bit of a change. Whatever Rachel Fortune had said to Joy, it had done a world of good.

Nancy put the wineglasses out. 'She's all right,' she

said. 'And us career girls must stick together –'
What's brought that on? Donna wondered. Nancy
struck a dramatic pose. 'Ahh,' she said. 'Nancy Garvey, Special Investigations Branch . . .' She flicked her
head, making her dangly earrings jangle.

'What's that . . . more money like?' Donna asked.
Some people had all the luck.

'Well, it's civvies. Joined-up writing. Every day different. You should try it.'

'Chance'd be a fine thing,' Joy said wistfully. She
stared at baby Matthew.

Donna patted her hand. 'It would teach them,
though, wouldn't it? – If they were here waiting for
us for once . . .' she let her voice trail off, thinking
about it. 'Make a nice change, eh pet?'

For a minute, nobody spoke. Then Nancy said,
'Let's have a nice glass of that wine, shall we?'

The sun set bloodily over the ridge where the platoon had come to a halt. Dave held the plastic drip
bottle up over Midnight the way the emergency
medic had shown him. It was the most and the least
he could do. The air was a little cooler now, as the
day died, but Midnight was still sweating. His eyes
flickered beneath the lids, and his hands lay loosely
on the sheet covering him.

You'll be all right, mate, Dave thought at him.
You've got to be, because if you die it'll be all my
fault. You wouldn't want that, would you, Midnight?

He looked around. The other men were standing
there silently, waiting for orders. Pereira was off to

one side, sitting crosslegged on the ground. From the angry, despairing look on his face, there was going to be hell to pay later.

The radio hissed as Tony Wilton tried to get through to the back-up vehicle. It crackled into life and he read out a set of map co-ordinates.

The medic closed his box of tricks and came over. He laid his hand on Midnight's forehead, then put two fingers against the pulse point at his throat. Not good. He chewed his lip for a second, then started loosening Midnight's clothing.

Wilton spoke into the radio headset. 'That's the nearest we can pinpoint our position, all right?' he said. 'Out.' He looked up. 'Ten minutes, Mr Pereira,' he said. 'They're sending an evac vehicle with a doctor on board.'

Doctor, Dave thought. It was serious, then. He'd somehow thought they'd say Midnight must be swinging the lead, that he'd just picked up a bit of a bug – like, malaria was a bit of a bug, say, or the plague. Wilton got up. He came over to help the medic.

'Oh God, what a mess,' Pereira muttered. 'I'm sorry about your birthday plans, Sergeant,' he added after a moment.

'Better things to worry about now, Mr Pereira,' Wilton said stiffly. He unbuttoned Midnight's shirt and yanked it open.

Dave stared down at Midnight. The laboured rasping of his breath cut the silence.

Donna picked up the bottle of wine and carefully

77

poured some more into Joy's glass, then Nancy's, then her own. Not much left, and this was the second bottle they'd gone through.

'Still,' Joy said brightly, 'worse things happen at sea.'

Joy by name, joyful by nature. Sometimes Donna wanted to slosh her one. But not tonight. Tonight it was just them against the world. Or at least, against their men, which came to much the same thing.

Nancy took a sip of her wine and scowled. 'I'll kill him,' she said. She paused to consider, then added, 'Slowly.'

'That's how Dave wants to go,' Donna said, 'slowly.' The others stared at her as if she'd said something stupid. 'In bed – a heart attack, you know – nearly there.' They still didn't get it. 'So he's got something to look forward to . . .' Well, all right, maybe it didn't make sense now, but it had when Dave had told her. 'I thought it was a good idea, me . . .' she finished.

Joy gave her a sly, sideways glance as she sipped her wine. Well, Donna thought, it probably wouldn't make much sense if you were married to Tony Wilton. What had Nancy said earlier? 'I bet he times it: forty-five seconds and that's your lot.' They had collapsed into giggles over the present they had chosen for him – a brightly coloured nude Donna thought would do nicely for the bedroom wall – and she had said, 'Aye pet – and when he rolls off he pulls out his clipboard and writes down, "Fusilier Joy shows promise".'

78

Just thinking about it made Donna start to laugh again. She stifled a giggle, and luckily for her the phone rang just then.

Joy got up to answer it. 'Bet this is them,' she said. 'This'd better be good.'

Better than Tony usually was, anyway, Donna hoped. She bit her lip to stop herself from laughing aloud. As Joy crossed the room to get the phone, Nancy leaned across the table and shook Donna's arm. She made a warning face at Donna.

'Hello,' Joy said, her annoyance obvious from her tone. This'll be good, Donna thought. She stopped laughing and swivelled round in her seat to listen. 'Oh! Mrs Fortune!' Joy said, her voice suddenly conciliatory. She shot Donna and Nancy a surprised glance.

'Yes,' she said uncertainly. And then, 'No.' And finally, 'Thank you . . .' She put the phone down.

'What is it,' Nancy asked.

'She reckons she's found me a job,' Joy said. 'In the nursery. They wanted her to do it – '

'Mrs Fleetstreet?' Donna said.

'That's what she said, more or less. But I could take Matthew, and it would give me a bit of money of my own . . .'

'How many shitty nappies do you have to change a day, then?' Donna asked. It didn't come out right. She had meant it to come out as a joke, but Nancy was glaring at her and so was Joy. It was all right for some, she thought: Nancy in the SIB, Joy working in the nursery. Where did that leave her, stuck at home all day alone? 'Sorry,' she muttered.

79

'Let's have a toast, shall we?' Nancy said. 'A toast to Joy and her shitty nappies.'

'Oh, thank you very much, Mrs Garvey,' Joy said, but she was laughing.

'Cheers,' Donna said. She downed her wine in one gulp.

It was pushing nine o'clock by the time the evac vehicle rattled into camp. The medics stretchered Midnight out of the van and slid him expertly on to a hospital trolley. Dave wasn't even allowed to hold the drip bottle this time. All he could do was follow along with Tony Wilton and Paddy Garvey as they trailed Lieutenant Pereira into the sick bay.

The doors of the sick bay slapped shut behind them. In the cold fluorescent lighting, Midnight looked much worse: his dark skin was shiny with cold sweat, and the oxygen mask didn't help.

'He looks at death's door,' Major Cochrane said from behind them.

Dave and Paddy Garvey turned as one. The Major looked furious.

'I'm sorry, sir,' Garvey said. 'They just slipped off.'

'We were too hot, sir,' Dave said. Paddy hadn't mentioned his name, but it was too much to hope that he'd get away with it. Not this time. Not with Midnight in that state. Not when his stupidity was at the back of it.

He heard footsteps behind him. Pereira came up. Dave stepped aside to make room for him to face Cochrane. 'It was my fault,' he said. 'I was in command, sir.'

Cochrane glared at them. 'You're experienced soldiers, for Christ's sake.' He wasn't talking to Pereira. 'Get off home, you two.'

Paddy and Dave came to attention for an instant, then left Pereira to it. As they went, they heard Pereira say, 'I was going for the record, sir. I thought that if I put the pressure on . . . stuck in with the lads . . .'

His voice trailed off just as Dave and Paddy got outside. Paddy started off down the path. Dave grabbed his arm with one hand. With the other, he kept the door open a fraction.

'– tried to tell me,' Pereira was saying. 'But I wouldn't listen.'

'Come on,' Paddy whispered. 'Haven't you caused enough tr–'

'Wait,' Dave hissed back. 'This'll be good.' He peered through the glass door.

'You allowed your men to swim in unknown water in the heat of the day,' Cochrane said. 'We should be glad you didn't wipe out the whole platoon.' He stalked – that was the only possible word for it – in the direction of the emergency room where the medics had taken Midnight.

Yes! Dave thought. This'll get Maradona off our backs for a while –

'Sir?' It was Tony Wilton's voice. 'They're not sure but they think Rawlings may have been poisoned, sir.'

Cochrane turned back to Pereira, who was staring at him like a mouse trying to face down a lion. 'You'd better get ready to face a regimental Board of Inquiry,' he said. His pale eyes bulged slightly, and red spots appeared high on his cheekbones. 'And you'll be bloody lucky if it ends there.'

Charming, Dave thought. The way Cochrane said it, anyone would think he was looking forward to it.

Chapter 4

The girls were not happy. The girls were, in fact, massively pissed off. Dave stood outside Tony Wilton's flat holding up the bottle of wine he and Paddy had bought as a peace offering. They'd stopped for that and to change into civvies – Dave was wearing a tangerine-coloured shirt, while Paddy had gone all cool and chosen black. Paddy hadn't wanted to stop even to do that much, but Dave had pointed out it would show the girls they were going to make up for everything, and have a really good night out. But Donna didn't seem to have got the message. She barred the doorway, scowling.

'Come on, pet,' Dave said. 'Let us in, man Donna. We've had a terrible time. We've been stuck out on that mountain – '

'Lost we were,' Paddy put in from behind him.

'And Midnight's half dead – ' He added. He dangled the bottle by its neck as a bribe.

Donna glared at him. 'Oh all *right*,' she said at last. 'But this had better be good.' She stood aside and let them in.

Nancy and Joy were sitting in the front room. It looked like they'd managed to get through the best part of a couple of bottles already. Paddy went over and gave Nancy a sloppy kiss. The joys of young love, Dave thought. He reached over and grabbed Donna round the waist.

'Don't you try it on, Dave Tucker,' she said, but she let him nuzzle the back of her neck.

'When you lot have quite finished, maybe someone could tell me what happened,' Joy said. 'And where my Tony is.'

'Mr Paella face, that's what happened,' Dave said. 'Got us lost going over the mountain instead of round it —'

'That and the rest,' Paddy added. He let Nancy go and started to take the cork out of the bottle. That's right, Dave thought. Rat me up. Paddy went on, 'And this dork and poor old Midnight skive off and go for a swim. Which is how come Midnight's banged up in hospital —'

'What on earth were you thinking about, Dave?' Joy demanded. 'There could have been anything in the water, and —'

'Doesn't sound like a bad idea to me,' Donna said. 'not in all that heat.' Dave grinned gratefully at her. She'd probably give him hell when they got home, but in public she was rock solid, behind him all the way.

Before he had to say anything, there was the rattle of a key in the front door, and a second later Tony walked in. He looked pale and angry; Dave wondered whether Pereira or Cochrane had had a go at him.

He stood up. 'Where've you been?' he asked. 'I'm starving —'

'They let me in to see Midnight,' Wilton said. 'Looks like he's going to be okay.'

'Great!' Joy exclaimed. 'You can take us all out then.' She got up and so did everyone else.

'Yeah, come on, ' Nancy said. 'We've been sitting here all night.'

Tony pulled a face like he'd just eaten a lemon. Joy ignored it. 'I'll just go and tell Mela – she is still in.'

'It's gone ten, Joy,' Tony said.

'Oh, come on, it's your *birthday*.' That was Donna.

Paddy went up to Tony and pinched his cheek. 'We're going to get ratted, my son,' he said.

'Has he got any civvies?' Donna asked.

'Course he has,' Joy said firmly.

'If you don't get those trousers off now – ' Donna said, and left the rest of the threat unspoken.

'She means it,' Dave said. You only ever made the mistake of underestimating Donna once. If you were really bright, you didn't underestimate her at all.

Tony had much the same problem with Joy. She jabbed him in the chest. 'Tony, do as you're told,' she said, punctuating her words with stabs of her finger. Then she swept out of the room, leaving a bewildered-looking Tony behind her.

A bit later on, they walked along the waterfront towards the steakhouse. The others were ahead of them. Dave slipped his hand into Donna's.

'Nice, this,' she said.

'Yeah,' he said. He couldn't think of anything to say. He just kept remembering Midnight lying on the

85

hospital trolley, with a drip in his arm and an oxygen mask on his face. 'It was all my fault, you know,' he said finally. Well, he had to tell someone. Maybe if he let the words out, they'd stop going round in his head.

'What was, pet?' Donna asked. She was staring out across the water, watching the harbour lights shimmer across its broken surface.

'Midnight. Us getting lost. I was too hot. I got Midnight to stay behind – the swim was my idea – '

'Oh, I see,' Donna said. 'Tied him up and forced him into the pool at gunpoint, did you?'

'Well no – '

'There you are then.' She squeezed his hand.

He'd expected her to call him all sorts. You never could tell with Donna. You just never could tell.

The *Chat Bleu* was just the way Donna liked a club to be – head-poundingly loud, packed with people, and just enough light to let you see your partner. Dave had cheered up a bit. He'd been miserable as sin earlier on, full of how he'd almost killed one of his best mates. But with a pint of lager to chase the wine he'd had earlier, he was doing all right. He grabbed her hand and led her out on to the floor. She took a last swig of her vodka and reached back to put the glass on the table as he pulled her into the dance. It was too fast for slow dancing, so she let go of his hand and let the music tell her how to move. She shut her eyes and let it go, and when she opened them again Dave was dancing right up close.

The music slowed. Dave reached for her, and she danced backwards, grinning, feeling the booze burn through her, letting her float above it all. That glint in his eye – she knew what he wanted, but he'd have to wait. She thought of later, of his body in the darkness and moonlight, and put her hand on his arm lightly, just enough to tease. He pulled her in, and she threw back her head and laughed, but when he moved to kiss her she laid a finger on his lips and moved away. Just as the music speeded up again, she heard Paddy – who had Nancy in a real dirty-dancing clinch – say, 'You get it wrapped up quick and come home to your old man –' She reached up and kissed him. He scooped her into his arms and carried her off in the direction of the bar. 'Gangway!' he yelled.

Donna threw her hands in the air and whirled, stamping in time to the suddenly rapid beat of the music. She put her hands on her hips and shimmied, knowing how tight her skirt was and just exactly what it would make Dave think about –

Suddenly, Tony Wilton's voice cut through the music. 'You leave my wife alone, got it?' he shouted.

Donna froze. Dave turned and pushed his way through the crowd. She followed him.

Joy was sitting on one of the leatherette banquettes, next to an American who was too pretty for his own good. Tony was sitting beside her, drinking bitter from a can and staring at his feet. He looked furious.

'He's not usually like this,' Joy said brightly.

'Usually,' Tony said, 'usually, I'm very quiet.' The

rage was building in his voice. 'Don't say boo to a goose – ' Suddenly he leaned across her, jabbing flat-handed at the American to punctuate his words, ' – but tonight I'm just not in the mood.'

Paddy was sitting next to him. He grabbed Tony's arm to haul him back, but the Sergeant pulled free and lunged at the Yank. 'You leave her alone or I'm gonna knock you out, got it?'

Joy twisted round, looking for some escape. Suddenly she grinned. 'Mr Pereira,' she said, sounding desperate.

He's a bit of all right, Donna thought – tall and dark, and vaguely Spanish-looking, though as Dave kept telling her, he was half Argentinian.

'Christ, just what we need,' Dave muttered from beside her. 'Mr wet-behind-the-ears Paella himself.'

'Alex,' the Lieutenant said. He was standing just behind the American.

'The boy wonder,' Tony sneered. He put his fingers to his lips and blew a parody of the Last Post.

Behind Pereira, the disco lights strobed. He grinned as if he really thought Tony were laughing with him, not at him. The American was another matter. He stared at Tony for a long moment. 'You really are determined to screw up the whole evening, aren't you?' he said. He looked pityingly at Joy, who in turn threw a desperate glance at Donna.

Paddy Garvey moved round behind Tony. Say something, Donna thought at Dave. Crack a joke, anything. It was what he was good at, making people laugh. But it was too late.

'Compared to this one, I'm a complete novice, right?' Tony said. He gestured at Pereira with the flat of his hand. 'He can screw up whole days, whole postings – ' Suddenly the anger was back in his voice. 'Whole. Bloody. Lives.' He spat the last few words out.

'Why don't we just sit down and enjoy ourselves?' Pereira said. He gestured to the seats.

He seemed canny enough, Donna thought. But she remembered that Dave had said that was his problem – that he wanted to get on with them so much he set himself up.

The American half turned to him. 'Sounds fine by me,' he said. He made to sit down.

For a second it seemed as if everything would be okay. Then Donna realized that Paddy hadn't moved, and that Dave had got himself between Joy and Tony.

'Oy, Yank!' Tony yelled. The American, still in the action of sitting down, turned round. 'I'll tell you when you can sit down, you Yankee bastard.' He shoved his middle finger in the air right in front of the good-looking American's face. He turned to Dave and Paddy and giggled, a high-pitched womanish sound that got right on Donna's nerves.

'Take a hike, asshole,' the American said. He turned away again.

'Who wants a drink?' Pereira said brightly. Jesus, Donna thought, he can't still think we're all going to sit down like long-lost cousins, can he? But he seemed to, because he went on, 'I'm buying!'

He started toward the bar just as Tony moved in

on him. He must have heard the Sergeant, because he turned back and squared off. Joy put herself between the two men. She was pink with embarrassment, and her eyes were bright with the beginnings of tears. 'Tony, you're making a complete prat of yourself,' she said.

Tony pushed her aside, but gently. 'Can't read a map,' he taunted, dragging out the words like a kid in a school playground. 'Got fresh air between his ears, but he thinks he knows it all.' Now his tone was matter of fact, as if he were stating the obvious. 'Don't you?'

Pereira looked at the floor for a second, as if he were really embarrassed. Paddy started to say something, but thought better of it.

'No,' Pereira said. 'But I thought I could benefit from your experience.' He was beginning to lose his temper.

Next to Donna, Dave made a slight snorting noise; so perhaps Tony did have a point after all.

'You didn't want to know –' Tony said.

'You were too busy sulking,' Pereira shouted. 'You wouldn't even give me a chance!' He leaned forward, and now his was the voice filled with contempt. 'And they said you were the best sergeant?'

Tony stared at him, apparently stunned; but whether it was because Pereira had finally had the guts to stand up to him, or because his superiors apparently thought that much of him, Donna couldn't say.

'I'm going now, Corporal Garvey,' Pereira said.

'Best thing, I think, sir,' Paddy said. He raised his glass, so that Pereira could see it but Tony couldn't, as if to distance himself from the ruckus.

Tony started to laugh, a horrible harsh sound that cut the disco music; but for a moment it looked as though real trouble had been avoided.

'Come on, pet,' Dave began. He started to pull Donna in the direction of the bar.

But just then the American turned round. 'My god,' he said. Tony stopped laughing. 'I feel sorry for you – ' He turned away.

You aren't the only one, Donna thought.

For a long moment, no one moved or said anything. Then Tony pushed past Paddy. Dave started towards him, but by the time he got there, the Sergeant had reached the American. He grabbed the man by the shoulder and spun him round.

'Be better off with you, would she?' He hauled back for a punch, but the man simply shoved him away, hard. Tony stumbled back and fell into the bank of chairs. He pushed back, shaking his head.

Just at that moment, Pereira realized what was going on. He turned back, glanced at the American, then started forward.

Tony got up. He turned and got off one good hard roundhouse punch – at Pereira, not the American. The Lieutenant staggered back and almost fell, but the American caught him. He moved forward, but Paddy got in the way.

Dave leapt at Tony and grabbed him from behind. Tony's mouth peeled back from his teeth in a grin that had nothing to do with amusement. He started to shake Dave off.

'You don't want to do this,' Dave said.

Pereira fingered his lip. For a moment the two men glared at each other. Then Pereira turned and left without saying anything.

Joy was pale. Her hand, which she was holding to her mouth, was shaking. She turned to Tony.

'Come on, pet,' Donna said. 'Let's get a drink down you. Leave these lads to sort their own testosterone poisoning out.'

There was only one good thing about it, Dave thought as he adjusted the wet cloth he had draped across his forehead, and that was that they weren't on duty this morning. He wriggled on his sunbed and sipped his orange juice. A couple of rather lovely young women tossed a beach ball around in the swimming pool. Too energetic by half, he decided. Not that he minded watching.

Paddy Garvey clambered out of the pool and tossed his towel on the sunbed next to Dave's. He had a face as long as a wet weekend – that would be because his Nancy had been posted up to the Free Territories. Poor sod, Dave mused. Mind you, the way Donna had been going on, maybe Paddy was the lucky one. Anyone would think he'd been the one that clipped old Paella-face, not Tony Wilton.

'Speak of the devil – ' he said aloud, as he spotted Tony making his way across the poolside.

'What?' Paddy said. He gave Dave a puzzled look, then hurried across to meet Tony.

The Sergeant was squinting against the sun, but if Dave was any judge his real problem was the brass band playing tarradiddles in his head. Dave was sure of that because it had taken five cups of coffee and several Paracetamol to get the ones in his own head to shut up. He vaguely remembered being asked to leave the *Chat Bleu*, then staggering down to the water's edge and taking a boat home, while the girls whined on the whole time. Including Donna. In fact, especially Donna – she hadn't been at all inclined to help him finish the night off properly when they got home . . .

'Hello Tyson,' Paddy said to Tony.

'How's it going?' Tony muttered.

Paddy glanced at Dave. 'Wonderful,' he said.

All right, all right, Dave thought. If you don't want me to listen, you should do your gassing somewhere else. He smiled at Tony, who pulled a sour face at him. 'Tell me about it,' he said. After a moment, he put his hand on Garvey's arm and the two of them turned slightly so they weren't facing Dave.

Charming, Dave thought. I suppose that means it's my turn to get the drinks in. But what the hell – whatever they didn't want him to hear was bound to be the most interesting gossip of all. He settled back to listen.

' - and see Julio in a minute,' Tony whispered. 'Listen, if it comes to it, buddy – if they want you to be a witness . . .'

'Oh, sure mate,' Paddy said. 'Mr Pereira attempted to stand his ground and Sergeant Wilton thumped him in self-defence . . . talk sense, Tone.'

Well, when you put it like that, it did sound bad, Dave thought. But there had to be another way of saying it – maybe they could say Pereira moved in on Joy or . . . nah, Donna would never go for it.

He suddenly picked his name out of the background clatter. 'Dave and Rawlings had permission for that swim – '

'What!' Tony exclaimed. He looked shocked.

'Yeah,' Paddy said. 'That poor sod's taken the can for us – letting Cochrane think he gave them permission, and not a word that we let them swan off. He's saved your bacon, mate. And mine. And theirs – not that they'll appreciate it . . .' He glared at Dave and went off in the direction of the changing-rooms.

That's charming, that is, Dave thought. Anyone would think we lied about it, when they didn't even bother to ask us.

He grinned at Tony, who was slumped against the wall. 'Drink?' he asked, raising his glass.

'Nah,' Tony said. 'I've got to go – ' He turned and walked away.

Joy was crying again. Nothing new there, Donna thought. She sat down next to her friend and tried to give her the cup of tea she had made. Joy's shoulders shook with the force of her crying.

'Come on, pet,' Donna said. She wished Nancy was there, but she had gone off on her assignment to the New Territories that morning. She would have known what to say. 'Crying won't mend it . . .' She laid her hand against Joy's back, but she just sobbed harder.

After a minute, Joy tried to wipe her eyes, but she had clutched her tissue so hard it had shredded.

'There you go,' Donna said, handing her another. Any more of this and she'd have to take out shares in Kleenex – she'd be on to a good thing.

Joy dabbed at her eyes, then took a long, ragged breath. 'He said he'd take me all over the world,' she said. She gave a little laugh, but there was nothing amused in it. 'I just didn't think he'd take me back home again so quick.' She spotted the tea, picked it up and took a sip. The cup rattled against the saucer as she put it back down. 'Well, he'll get shipped back to military prison now, won't he?'

'Oh no, pet – he'll probably just lose his stripe,' Donna said, hoping to cheer her up; but then she realized she was being a bit optimistic, and before she could stop herself she'd added, 'or all of them.' Joy gave her a look that could have soured cream. 'Well, he might . . . !' she said. No point looking for the light at the end of the tunnel when it was probably just an oncoming train, she thought.

Joy didn't say anything, just sipped her tea. When she had finished it, she banged it down on the coffee table. 'Just when it was all coming right . . .' she said. She let her voice trail off as if she were thinking of a life she would not now have the possibility of leading. 'A chance for me to get a job, a whole place to explore . . . and then that prat goes and wrecks it all – '

Donna grinned sympathetically. She started to say that Tony wasn't the only prat around, but stopped herself. There wasn't any point – Joy was crying

again. She sighed heavily, and went into the kitchenette to start the washing-up left over from the night
before.

She was almost finished when Tony arrived. She
heard his key turn in the lock and went and stood in
the doorway between the kitchenette and the living-
room. He looked a bit ragged round the edges – pale
and with sore eyes, and for once even his uniform
looked just slightly rumpled. Joy looked up at him.
Her mascara was smeared across her cheeks, and
light glinted off the tears that coated her face.

Tony walked slowly across to her. He seemed to
notice Donna for the first time, and made a motion
with his head that clearly said, 'Hop it.' For a second
she lingered – just long enough to see him go on his
knees in front of Joy and take both her hands in his.

Donna went back into the kitchenette. She started
to make some more tea – they were going to need it,
she was certain – but she couldn't help overhearing.

'It's all right, darling,' Tony said. His voice was
utterly tender, and like nothing Donna had ever
imagined coming from him. 'Pereira didn't report
me – '

'What?' Joy said. Donna could imagine the way her
eyes would go wide with shock.

'Said it was on him – a birthday present – '

Joy laughed. There was a scuffling sound. Donna
poked her head round the door. Sure enough, they
were snogging away like a couple of teenagers.

'You'll not be wanting tea, then?' she asked.

Joy broke off. 'Please,' she said.

'Coffee for me, please, Donna,' Tony said. He squeezed Joy's hand.

Well, Donna thought. Tony wasn't the only prat around, but on the other hand he wasn't the biggest one, either.

Dave hated hospitals. It was the smell of them – got right to the back of your throat, and for days after, all you could taste was disinfectant. Still, they couldn't not go to see Midnight, not after all the trouble there'd been.

'Good news about Tony, eh?' he said, as they walked along the cream-walled corridor.

'No thanks to you two,' Paddy said.

'Well, no harm done – worse things happen at sea,' Dave said.

'Makes me glad I didn't join the navy,' Paddy answered, but there was almost a smile playing round his lips. 'Mind you, it could have been nasty – not least for our Mr Pereira.'

'What? Him? With his connections?' Surely Paddy didn't think old Julio had ever been in any real danger? They rounded a corner and pushed through a pair of plastic swing doors. 'Slap on the wrist, him, if that. You mark my words.'

'Not if Cochrane had had his way – he was all hot for a regimental Board of Inquiry till Tony stepped in and admitted how you two skived off behind Pereira's back. Poor bastard was all set to carry the can for all of us.'

'Oh aye,' Dave said. 'Well, if he hadn't been mustard to get us on that speed march –'

'Shut it, Dave,' Paddy said. He picked up a bit of speed, so that Dave fell a little way behind. 'You were wrong and you know it – '

'Oh come on – ' Dave started, but by that time they were in the ward. He shrugged behind Paddy's back and hurried to catch up. By the time he got to Midnight's bed, Paddy was already deep in conversation.

'Yeah,' Midnight said. He was stripped to the waist and he looked very pleased with himself as he lay back in the bed, a self-satisfied grin on his face. 'I got electrolytes in my blood,' he ticked the list off on his fingers as he went. 'Salt and . . . . what's the other thing?'

'Bullshit?' Dave supplied.

'I nearly died, ' Midnight said. When that didn't work, he added, 'Twice.' Just at that moment a nurse, pretty in a plump, blonde kind of way, came to refill Midnight's water jug. 'Thanks, love,' he said to her. She turned and reached across him to fluff his pillows up. 'This is the one that sponged me down,' he said from behind her. Oh yeah, Dave thought. 'All over,' Midnight finished.

Dave glanced at Paddy. 'All right for some,' he mouthed. Then he added aloud, 'I drank some of that water – ' The nurse turned and grinned at them. Very nice, Dave thought. He rolled his eyeballs up and belly-flopped none too gracefully across the bed, to be followed an instant later by Paddy.

Any minute now, Dave thought, waiting for the nurse even though she obviously didn't believe a word of it. Then Midnight yelled, 'Nurse! Nurse!'

Dave looked up. Midnight had his hand clamped across his mouth. He let it down long enough to yell, 'I'm going to be sick, nurse!'

The nurse hurried over, clutching a kidney bowl. Midnight turned so she had to lean across him. He put his arm round her, then let his hand hover above her waist. Dave grinned. You wouldn't dare, my son, he thought at his friend. He was right, but Midnight let his hand drift slowly down to her bottom and, still without actually touching her, he pretended to have a good pinch.

'Lucky – ' Dave hissed; but Midnight put a finger to his lips, and after that there wasn't much they could do but leave.

It was embarrassing seeing Mr Paella again, Dave reckoned – Tony too, come to think of it. After all, if things had gone differently, one or both of them might have been out of the army or at least with a note on their permanent record.

Just as well they were up for inspection when it happened. 'Guard! Guard, '*shun*!' Paddy shouted as Tony and Pereira came up to the guard-house. He turned crisply with a stamp of his heels, and said, 'Guard formed and ready for inspection, sir.'

Dave sucked his belly in and tried to be a good little soldier. It was no use. He just kept looking at Pereira's anxious little hamster face, and Tony's bulging blue eyes, and it made him want to laugh.

He'd been the same at school – the first one in trouble, then the first one in double trouble for laughing at the teachers when they told him off.

'Corporal Garvey, you'll have an early-morning convoy to book out,' Pereira said. He was very serious – subdued even.

It made Dave want to laugh all the more.

It was Midnight – back on duty and full of bull about his beautiful nurses and what they'd had to do for him – who saved his bacon. He wobbled around in position, then rolled his eyes up and started to fall sideways. Dave caught him.

'What the bloody hell's going on here?' Tony said.

'Oh no!' Dave said. 'It's a relapse!' Much better to get into trouble for this than laughing at your commanding officer.

'Tucker, leave him,' Tony said.

Dave let Midnight go. He fell to the side, hitting the floor dramatically – and a bit obviously, Dave thought – as he landed.

Dave bent over him, and slapped him lightly on both cheeks. He squinted up in the direction of Tony and Pereira. 'He's not been the same, sir, since that do on the speed march – '

Tony, evidently not impressed, came slowly across the parade ground. He squatted down beside them.

'I need a nurse, sir,' Midnight moaned. 'That blonde one will do – '

'You'll need more than a nurse in a minute, Rawlings,' Tony said, 'to extract this stick.' He glared at Dave and jabbed his chrome-tipped swagger stick towards him. Dave let himself grin at last. It didn't last. 'I'll have fifty press-ups from the both of you,' Tony said quietly. 'And I'll have them now.' Dave

100

managed to get the smile off his face. Not fast enough. 'NOW!' Tony screamed.

He stood up. Midnight and Dave scrambled to their feet. 'Loud count, Corporal Garvey,' Tony said.

'Certainly, Sergeant,' Paddy said. Dave would have sworn he sounded pleased about it, but he didn't have time to think about that, or about the fact that Pereira and Tony had gone off chatting together like old mates. He was too busy keeping his belly up and his dips low.

Chapter 5

The Chinese border was hell — a moist green hell of dripping vegetation that stank of decay and stagnant water and a heady mix of unidentifiable spices. Dave crept forward between Tony and Foster, another squaddie he didn't know very well, with Paddy on the end of the line. Somewhere ahead of them, there was a wall of razor wire. Somewhere behind them there was a watch-tower, where the duty lookout scanned the jungle with binoculars, ready to inform Pereira — who was back at the Operations Room with Midnight — if he saw anything at all. And then Pereira would radio whichever patrol was closest to the sighting so they could move in.

That was the theory. Just at that moment, Dave wasn't terribly interested in it. He had his mind on other things. He crept forward and shoved incautiously at an overhanging branch —

What had she said, last night on the phone? 'You don't care — ' He'd tried to protest, to say he was sorry if she was lonely, that he'd be back soon, but she'd been in no mood to listen, not that she ever was . . .

— the branch snapped like a gunshot in the jungle quiet. 'For pity's sake,' Tony hissed.

'Sorry, Sarge – ' Dave whispered round a mouthful of gum. Get a grip, he told himself. Closest thing they'd seen to action for months, and what was he thinking about? A row with his wife. Not that he didn't have cause to dwell on it. He batted at a mosquito. The camo smearing his face did nothing to keep the little buggers away, and neither did the repellent spray they'd been issued with. You'd think this early in the morning they'd be sleeping or something, but dawn or dusk, it was all the same to the mozzers of Hong Kong.

Tony raised his binoculars to his eyes and muttered something.

What had Donna said? Exactly? 'It isn't you that has to carry the can. It never is.' Now where had he heard that before? He stared at the jungle, trying to spot the razor wire through it.

Paddy took a drag of his cigarette. 'Millions of reds over there. The thin khaki line over here,' he said. He was wearing a green scarf wrapped pirate-style round his fair hair, and over it the radio headset. Somewhere, a bird chirred up out of the trees, squawking in protest at the noise.

'Ready to take 'em on with our bare hands,' Dave deadpanned. He'd long since found out that it was the best way to find out whether Paddy was taking the piss or not. You could never tell with him. One minute he'd be all gung-ho for the army, making out it was everything to him – except his Nancy of course – and the next minute he'd be up for any laugh going. Not this time, though. Not from the disgusted look he exchanged with Tony. Well, just this once Dave wasn't going to back down. 'They only want a job,' he said. 'They only want to get over a poxy wall to get a poxy job.'

The others said nothing. Dave chewed his gum. Why was it so hard for them to understand? Sure, they hadn't come out of school in the north-east, with one card on the job-centre noticeboard a month – in a good month. They maybe hadn't looked round and known their lives would revolve around a fortnightly giro cheque and the housing benefit for ever, unless they did something. Or maybe they had. He'd never really asked them why they joined up, just taken it for granted that they'd had their reasons – which, he'd assumed, were pretty much like his reasons.

Till now, when they couldn't understand that you could want a job so badly you'd hurl yourself at forty feet of razor wire and face a battalion of armed men to get it. His hand fell to the heavy bamboo baton at his side, and he wondered if the Chinese knew the soldiers weren't issued with firearms, and whether it would have made any difference to them if they had.

You'd have to do it, he thought. If you had a family to look after, you'd want to – maybe to find ways of sending money back to them. Donna: last night she'd said he didn't care, that if he cared he'd leave the army and find a job that wouldn't take him away so much, that wouldn't mean she was away from her mam. But she knew how hard that would be – what was there on Tyneside now, to replace the old ship-yards? A job in a heritage museum, maybe? But not for him, not with his couple of CSEs. But he'd have to do something to make sure things were different –

'Get a bloody move on, Tucker,' Paddy said. 'At this rate, they could have the whole of the Red Army over that wall before we get there.'

'All right, all right,' Dave said. He followed Tony, who picked his way through the dense undergrowth for what seemed like hours until they came to a shallow, slow-moving stream. They were halfway across it when Paddy's radio crackled into life.

He said something into it, and though Dave knew Midnight must be on the other end, he couldn't make out what was being said.

False alarm, probably, he thought. They should be so lucky. It all depended what you wanted, he supposed.

A few minutes later they were splashing and crashing down the stream at the double, holding their batons awkwardly above their heads, out of force of habit, like they were rifles. Spray dashed in Dave's face and he screwed up his eyes and could barely see, but that was okay because all he had to do was keep going in a straight line with Paddy's back in front of him, and in any case the greatest danger was that he would lose his footing in the thin slime and pebbles of the stream bed.

Tony stumbled and fell forward, then regained his footing, but now he was chest deep in the greasy water. Paddy moved on, slowly. 'It shelves,' he said. Dave followed him, testing the stream bed cautiously with the point of his toe, and found that, sure enough, it fell steeply away. He sighed and went on, but was still not ready for the cold slap of the water on his hot skin.

'Get a bloody move on,' Tony said, 'or we'll all catch our deaths.'

They headed for the far shore, but now they could only move slowly, forcing their way through the stream. Then they were out the other side, clambering through the ferns and long wet grass, and trying to get to the cover of the trees, and most of all to spot the Chinese before they were spotted themselves.

Dave's sodden uniform clung to him; the soused fabric was heavy, and he could already feel the wet leather of his boots rubbing against his feet, socks or no. He'd have blisters the size of football pitches tonight, that was for sure.

Tony put up a cautioning arm. 'Shh!' he said unnecessarily. Dave tried to look into the sun. What had the Sergeant seen? All Dave could make out was the glare of sunlight on water, and a tangle of vegetation.

False alarm, he thought again; but he remembered the panic in Donna's voice, and he knew it wasn't so.

Tony signalled for them to crouch, and he did so, forcing himself to concentrate. Got to do well now, he thought. Earning for three ... he suppressed a grin. Tony was signalling them to move off to the left, and Dave suddenly wanted to do a good job – no, a brilliant job – and let them see he was better than the fuck-up they thought he was.

Paddy put his hand to his earpiece, then whispered, 'Thirty metres and closing.'

Tony nodded. They moved out in silence. Here we go, Dave thought. His foot caught in a knot of grass, and he put his hand out to save himself.

It took a heartbeat for what he was feeling to register: there was something warm and slightly rubbery under his hand. He looked down. The flat white eye of a dead pig stared up at him. He cried out, a harsh scream that cut the silence and lurched back; even as he did so a maggot, pus yellow and as thick as his thumb, crawled out of the pig's nostril, coiled and stretched in the warm air, then dropped slowly to the ground.

'Oh Jesus,' he said, gulping for breath, 'I'm sorry, I'm sorry.'

'You stupid –' Tony Wilton began, but what else he had to say was lost in the explosion of noise from the bushes as the Chinese illegals crashed away from them. 'Shit!' Tony exclaimed. 'Get after them, quick.'

Then there was no more time for apologies or explanations as they all charged after the intruders. Dave – still recovering from the pig – found himself bringing up the rear as they ran, swinging their batons to clear a way through the undergrowth.

'Got to do this,' he muttered to himself, letting the words pound out of him as his feet slammed into the soft jungle mulch. 'Got to, for Donna and me and – '

Then there was no more time for thinking about it. Up ahead of him, the others had come out into a clearing. They were circling a handful of intruders, arms out ready to grab them if they tried to push past, like kids playing bulldog in the schoolyard. Then the game was on and his mates had tackled the Chinese, brought them down with rugby tackles that would have done Will Carling proud. Impossible to see much at this distance, but they didn't seem to be doing too badly. Leave some for me, he thought; just a little bit of glory, to help him on his way to that first stripe, the one that would turn the army into a proper career instead of just a job.

He tried to put on a burst of speed, then found himself shoulder charging a pair of illegals of his own, who had come out of nowhere, it seemed. Someone moaned. They went down. He didn't. Without thinking about it, he raised the baton ready to roundhouse them with it if they tried to get up. But they barely moved.

He stared down at them. A man, maybe Dave's own age, with a wound in his leg you could put your hand in, a wound that was already attracting flies. His mouth stretched round a scream that he simply refused to let out. But the other one – the other one was just a kid, five or six, if that. They lay staring up at Dave, all terrified eyes and blue-black hair and bones that stuck through their skin they were so skinny.

Slowly, the man raised his hands, as if he thought Dave's baton was really a rifle. The kid looked at him, then did the same. Dave could see his chest, thin as a bird's, labouring under his filthy rag of a tee-shirt.

'Oh hell,' Dave muttered. He heard himself telling Paddy: All they want is to get over a poxy wall so they can get a poxy job –

You'd have to, wouldn't you? If you had a kid to look after, you'd do what you could, what you had to, whatever it took.

He knew he would.

He stared at them a second longer, then at the rest of the patrol. They were still busy. Dave realized they'd only been standing there for a matter of seconds. If he brought them in, they'd be tossed in some stinking hole of a prison – split up for sure – and God only knew what the Chinese authorities would do to them. If it had been just the man, it would have been different. But the kid . . . he couldn't do that to the kid.

'Go,' he whispered to them. They just lay there, and he said again, more emphatically, 'Go!' and gestured at the jungle with his baton. They scrambled to their feet, and he thought: This is daft, this is impossible. There's still time; all I have to do is grab the kid and the bloke'll stop. But he didn't move, and they ran off into the undergrowth without even looking back at him.

He turned and looked at the others. They were cuffing the illegal immigrants they had caught. They hadn't seen him, he was pretty sure of that. He trotted over to them, and it was only when he got up close and saw the expression on the face of one of the prisoners that he realized that anyone had seen what had happened.

They started the long march back to the pick-up vehicles. The prisoners trudged along in the middle of the group, with their shoulders slumped and unable even to swat the mosquitoes that buzzed around them because their hands were cuffed behind their backs to the bamboo batons Dave and the others had been carrying.

Dave wondered, idly, whether any of them had family – wives, kids – back in China. Maybe they'd planned to send money back to them. Maybe they'd even have managed to do it. More likely the poor little tykes would have grown up on the streets, without even the benefit of your friendly local social services to take them in.

Tell me about it, he thought to himself savagely as they came to a bridge across the river.

What chance were those kids going to have now? At least the one he'd let go would have a chance. The older one – his brother, maybe, or father – would do his best for him.

You'd have to do your best if you had a kid to look after, no doubt about it.

A group of fish-farmers had started across the bridge from the other side. They were wrapped in layers of waterproofs, with sacks of heaven knew what slung over their shoulders; they wore coolie hats and, even in the boiling heat, gloves and boots. The smell of them – rotten fish and body odour – arrived before they did.

Well, it was a job, Dave supposed. Better than nowt.

Paddy was speaking to him. He realized just in time to catch the end of what the blond corporal said. 'That's the job you should put in for – ' Dave raised an eyebrow at him. 'Fish-farming. You've got all the gear. And the smell.'

'Hurr hurr hurr,' Dave chuckled, cartoon style. No one laughed.

One little mistake and you never got forgiven, that was the truth.

'Look, I couldn't help it,' he said as they got to the far side of the bridge. 'It was a dead pig. It was looking at us — ants crawling all over it. Maggots.' He turned back to Paddy. 'You ever felt a dead pig?'

'No,' Paddy answered in that dry way he had. 'But I've lived with a few.'

From the expression on his face, Dave thought, there wasn't any doubt who he meant.

Later — it seemed like half a lifetime later to Dave — they arrived back at the camp. Tony went off to process the prisoners. Foster suggested getting a beer first and shower later, and to hell with the stink, and Dave was about to agree — he could put up with it if Foster could — when he realized that Paddy had shot off somewhere.

Still pissed off, Dave thought. Bloody typical, just when he wanted to talk to him.

'I'll see you later,' he said, and headed off down the corridor at a trot, hefting his pack over one shoulder as he went.

Shower, that would be Paddy, he thought. Sure enough, as he turned the corner he saw the Corporal heading into the locker-rooms. He slowed to a walk, wondering what he could say. He wanted to make it right – to prove that it wasn't just another case of him screwing up, the way they all thought. And the other stuff too, of course.

He kicked the locker-room door open and swung his pack down on one of the benches. He glanced towards the shower room, but there was no noise from it. He had to be in the bog then.

'Paddy?' he yelled. He walked down the line of cubicles, slamming the flat of his hand against each one. 'Paddy? I know you're in – '

'Piss off, Dave,' Paddy yelled.

'Sorry about the pig and that,' Dave said. That was the easy part. He slumped with his back to the cool wood of the wall next to Paddy's cubicle, and sighed. How did you say what he had to say next, when you couldn't even think about it because it made your balls shrivel and your gut knot, and the one person in the world that you should be able to talk to didn't want to know anyway? There wasn't an easy way to say it, but he said it anyway. 'We're having a kid.' Silence from the other side of the door. Say something, man Paddy, he thought desperately. But there was still only silence. 'Donna and me,' he said at last.

He threw his head back to rest against the door. It felt too heavy for his shoulders, as if it were made of lead. There was so much else he had to say, and he knew he couldn't say any of it. Not even to Paddy. Not and hold his head up.

The door rattled, then opened a crack. Paddy, sitting on the toilet, peered through it. He looked as if someone had just rammed him in the belly with the butt end of a rifle. 'You what?' he said.

112

'I'm gonna have a baby,' Dave said; but he thought, I'm going to be a dad . . . 'Great, isn't it?' He turned to look at Paddy, who was staring up at him with a look of near horror on his face.

The big Corporal reached up and thumped him lightly on his arm. 'Yeah,' he said. 'If you say so, mate.' He sat back down and closed the door.

Thanks for the vote of confidence, like, Dave thought.

'How's Donna taken it?' Paddy's voice was muffled by the wooden door.

The sixty-four thousand dollar question, Dave thought. The one he'd been dreading. And avoiding asking himself all morning. 'Oh, dead pleased,' he said; but he couldn't even put enough enthusiasm into it to fool himself, let alone Paddy. 'Well, she will be,' he said. If he said it often enough, it might even be true. 'Never thought I'd have my own family,' he said. 'I've never had me own family – ' Not unless you counted Tyneside social services. What would it be like? A kid – a boy, his son – to take to football matches. Something flashed through his mind, like a snatch of long-forgotten memory, of himself and a young lad kicking a ball around on a patch of vivid green grass, with Donna waiting somewhere out of sight, ready with a pot of tea and a plate of butties. Oh, it would be grand, if only –

Paddy cut into his thoughts. 'I'm very happy for you.' He sounded about as happy as Donna had when she'd told him. 'Now sod off and leave me in peace.'

'Right,' Dave said. One more thing. He'd said all the rest. He might as well say the last part of it. 'Only, I want to get my first stripe.' No response. 'You know. Start getting somewhere.'

Still nothing.

You'd have thought Paddy would understand. If you had a kid, you had to do the best you could for it. And Donna too, of course. 'Cheer her up about the baby, I thought. Only she's dead pleased really. Underneath, you know.'

If he said it often enough, maybe it would be true.

Donna sat cross-legged by the window. The rising sun poured fire into the sky, but she wasn't in the mood for beautiful sunsets. She was holding the phone to her ear, and she was shaking.

'A bit more consideration wouldn't go amiss –' said the voice on the other end. Mrs Gilbert. Her mam's neighbour.

'I just wanted to speak to me mam,' Donna said for what seemed like the hundredth time, but which might only have been the tenth. 'I thought you could bang on the wall and get her –' The old bat had done it often enough before, after all.

'It's two o'clock in the morning, Donna. You should –'

'Well, I didn't know it was that bloody time, did I?' Donna cut in. She was shouting, and there'd be hell to pay when she did speak to her mam, but she didn't care.

'You just watch your tongue when you speak to me –'

'And the same to you, you old bag,' Donna snarled. She slammed the phone down.

She wasn't crying, she told herself. She put her hand to her eyes and wiped away mascara-blackened tears. But she wasn't crying. She was just angry.

Chapter 6

Here we go, Dave thought. This is where Tucker and the pig goes down in military history . . . He stood to attention with the rest of the platoon as Colonel Fortune and Major Cochrane came out on to the balcony in front of the Operations building. Cochrane stayed there, but the Colonel came partway down the steps to take the salute.

He stared at the men for a long moment, then said to Tony Wilton, 'What exactly was it that fouled up the ambush? Remind me?'

'A pig, sir.' The men laughed. Tony wasn't amused. He turned to them and screamed, 'Shut up.' Then to the Colonel, 'Gave us a bit of a fright, sir.'

'Frightening sort of a pig, was it?'

'Big, sir. Noisy. Very fast-moving.'

Colonel Fortune didn't seem impressed with that. He stared into the distance and said, 'Very good, Sergeant. You're getting better at it. What sort of pig was it?'

'A bit of a dead one, sir,' Tony said. This time he was almost smiling himself, and when everyone laughed, he didn't bawl them out. Maybe he'd realized there wasn't going to be any comeback, Dave decided.

'My God,' Colonel Fortune said, shaking his head but obviously amused. He started up the concrete stairs. 'All yours, Bob,' he said to Major Cochrane.

Cochrane leaned on the railing that surrounded the balcony. 'All right, lads,' he said. 'You finally caught our Chinese friends, but I don't want anymore cock-ups like that.' He paused. Dave thought, I don't want any more cock-ups either. Not if I'm going to get my jack-stripe . . . 'Last British regiment on border duty ever,' Cochrane continued. 'So let's make bloody sure we're the best one yet.' He paused. 'Well done.' He said it as if he resented having to say it. Not free with his praise, the Major, Dave thought; and unlike the Colonel, he didn't much make you want to earn it from him, either. 'Carry on,' Cochrane said to Pereira.

They saluted, then Pereira said, 'Wives' barbecue squad – get to it! Sergeant?'

Wilton told them to fall out, but Dave was busy thinking about Donna – what he'd say to her, how pleased she'd be to see him – how happy she'd be about the baby, now she'd had time to think about it.

She would be pleased. Surely.

Too sodding hot, that was the trouble with Hong Kong, Donna thought, even by the sea where you might hope for a bit of a breeze. But the day was dead calm, and she felt as if she were smothering in the heat. She strolled along next to Nancy clutching her white shoulder bag and wishing the other woman would just hop it and leave her alone.

But she wouldn't, of course. 'I called for you last night,' she said.

'I was out,' Donna answered, hoping Nancy would leave it at that.

'Where?' Nancy demanded.

To Donna it was as if she were being poked at with a stick. 'That club in – ' She started. Then she realized what she was saying. God, no. If that got back to Dave, there'd be hell to pay. 'Well if you must know, I've got a job.' Not that he'd be much better pleased with that. Still, might as well be hanged for a major gaffe as a minor indiscretion, she thought. 'That's where I'm going now,' she said. 'To collect my pay.'

'That's great – ' Nancy said.

'Don't tell Dave. He'd kill us,' Donna said, suddenly realizing the news would be all over married quarters about ten minutes after Nancy got back. 'It's just till he gets back – in a British pub. Evenings.'

'Donna!' Nancy said. 'All the wives think you're out on the town every night – '

Just typical, that was. Just bloody typical – didn't have enough to think about, so all they could do was gossip. 'Oh, who gives a monkey's about them old slags?' she demanded. They were just jealous – they'd get themselves jobs in a second if they had the nerve. But that wasn't what good little army wives did. 'He goes to the border and it's "Cheerio Donna, be a good girl for six weeks."'

For a second it looked as if Nancy wanted to say something to her – something she maybe thought Donna wouldn't want to hear. In the end what she did say was, 'You are coming today, aren't you?'

Great. Bloody brilliant, Donna thought. 'Dinner with the army in the middle of nowhere? Hold us back.' Nancy grinned at her. It isn't bloody funny, Donna thought. She wanted to cry, but that just wasn't what she did. 'I'm going out of my head with it all, Nance,' she said.

Nancy patted her arm and they walked along in silence.

It was all right for Nancy, Donna thought. She didn't know what that *all* was.

The observation tower was a platform on forty-foot-high stilts, made from metal tube, corrugated iron and wire netting, and camouflaged with dead leaves and branches to reduce its visibility. From its top you could see for miles into the jungle on the Chinese side of the border, even without binoculars; but Dave was concerned with something a bit closer to home – Colonel Fortune, who was sharing the platform with him. When Tucker first joined up, he'd been his runner; but that was long ago, and these days the only time he got close to the man was when he was in trouble – which was far too often for comfort.

Now, the Colonel stood next to him, watching the jungle on the other side of the border. He lowered the binoculars and handed them to Tucker. 'Who are they?'

Tucker raised the bins, hoping he'd know the answer. Had to impress the old man. Just had to, after this morning. Through the lenses he saw a gaggle of Chinese men and women with baskets on their backs; they were making their way between a cluster of dilapidated bamboo and corrugated iron huts, and the river, where half a hundred white ducks swam. He'd watched them go and come back before, so at least he knew the answer to one question. He had to stop himself sighing aloud with relief. 'Duck farmers, going off, sir. They'll be back in a couple of hours.'

'What would you do if you saw some of them walk along the track and then they vanished, down there in the scrub?' Fortune asked.

Twenty bloody questions, Tucker thought. But he knew the answer to this one too. 'Tell the Ops Room, sir. Let them decide if it was anything important.'

'Good,' the Colonel said. 'Don't take any chances. If we miss them here they end up in Hong Kong with no jobs, no homes, no nothing.'

Bloody hell, Dave thought. He knows. He *knows*.

But when the Colonel spoke again, it was to change the subject. He stepped forward and leant on the waist-high railing surrounding the observation platform. 'That business with the pig, Tucker. What the hell were you using for brains?'

Dave couldn't see his face, but he didn't need to – it was obvious the old man was annoyed. He realized that he was ashamed of himself, not just embarrassed the way he would be if the other lads were ragging him about it. 'Yeah, I'm a bit pissed off about that myself,' he said. Then, before he could stop himself, he found himself saying, 'Me and Donna's having a kid – '

The Colonel looked round with a shocked expression on his face – much the same one Paddy Garvey had worn when Dave told him. 'What?'

'Sir,' Dave confirmed. 'Well, I want to start getting somewhere, sir – up the ranks and that.' He looked at the Colonel, whose look of shock had turned into one of amusement. 'No, I mean it, sir.' He did too – he'd show them, now he'd set his mind to it. No more Tucker the screw-up, he thought. From now on, he was going to be the best.

Colonel Fortune glanced at the ground, dizzyingly far below. 'You shouldn't say that to a man at the top of a forty-foot ladder – ' Dave didn't quite get that, and before he could figure it out, the Colonel said, 'Congratulations. Nip down and see the padre.' Before Dave could say anything, he took the binoculars. 'Go on,' he urged. 'I'll spell you.'

Dave came briefly to attention. 'Sir,' he said, and started down the long ladder. He really didn't want to talk to the padre, but an order was an order. What else had he joined the army for?

He found the padre drinking tea under an awning near the headquarters building.

'Come on in and sit down, Tucker,' he said, waving at a camp-stool. In the background an electric fan whuffed, and an old-fashioned kettle hissed to itself as it boiled on a primus stove nearby. 'Now, what can I do for you?'

'Colonel Fortune said I should talk to you, sir – ' He looked away, across the camp and beyond, where the green folds of hills fell steeply away into the distance. Somewhere in that direction was the sea, and across the bay the army camp, where his Donna was waiting for him. If she would only wait. And then there it was again, tumbling out before he could stop himself. 'It's my Donna. She's pregnant. We're going to have a baby.' The padre handed him a cup of tea. It was pale green, in the Chinese fashion, and there was no milk in it. A few large leaves floated lazily near the surface. Dave looked at it suspiciously for a second, then sipped it. It was very good. 'At least, we are if . . .' he let his voice trail off. How could you tell a priest what he thought Donna might have in mind? 'She wants it kept quiet,' he said at last. 'I feel like telling everyone, me.'

The padre picked up the pot and swished the tea round in it. 'Take an old man's advice,' he said. 'Don't. Go at her pace. I'll get one of the other wives to look after her.' He paused for a sip of tea. 'Who do you think?'

'I don't know,' Dave said, thinking of the explosion there'd be the second one of the women tried any such thing. 'Funny about people, my Donna. I can't get through to her.'

'Just be nice to her when she gets here,' the padre said. He pursed his lips as if trying to remember something. '"Husbands, love your wives and do not be harsh with them",' he said, as if he were announcing the reading in mass. 'Colossians three, eighteen.'

Dave stared at him for a second. A slight, sly, smile played round the older man's mouth. 'You made that up,' Dave said, accusingly.

For an answer, the padre grinned broadly, then sipped his tea.

* * *

The British pub where Donna worked was called 'The Jouster Inn'. Every morning the manager, Pete Lewis, dragged a full-size suit of armour outside, to stand guard next to the fake portcullis that decorated the main door. Every night after closing, he dragged it back inside again. Donna reckoned what with the humidity it was a wonder the thing hadn't turned into a pile of rust long since, but he explained that it had been specially lacquered when he'd had it made, a couple of years ago.

Bloody typical she'd thought at the time – the suit of armour was as authentic as the rest of the bar, with its plastic oak beams that didn't hold the ceiling up, and its so-called pewter mugs that hung on hooks behind the bar, but which the customers weren't allowed to use. Well, what did you expect from some-one who had an accent as English as Crocodile Dundee's?

Not that she cared about that. In fact, all she really wanted at that moment was to get her money off Pete's wife and go. Which she did, and then went out blinking into the sun. Hong Kong dollars might not be worth much, but at least you got a nice thick wodge of them.

Pete was still manhandling St George – that was Donna's pet name for the suit of armour – into posi-tion. She smiled at him, and he nodded sourly at her from behind his dark glasses. Quite deliberately, she paused and started counting her money. Didn't want him thinking he could put one over on her. She thought he was going to say something, but just then an American who had pestered her all the night before wandered up.

'Well, look who's here.' He was wearing sunglasses too – posey aviator-style ones. He took them off as he spoke to her. 'Where'd you go last night?' he asked, angling round so she couldn't avoid him without being obviously rude. He was plain and pasty-faced, balding and skinny, but with just the start of a beer belly. She wasn't surprised he wore the glasses.

'I finished midnight,' Donna said. It was the truth. 'I went home to me lonely little bed.' She said it sarcastically, to shut him up; but as soon as the words were out she could see it had been a bad move. You could almost see the gears whirring around in his brain as he worked out the possibilities – and his chances.

Well, fat chance, chum, she thought.

'Hey, how about that? Me too!' he said.

Donna looked at him – not just the hair and the belly, but the sweat-stained Hawaiian tee-shirt and the too-eager smile on his face. 'Fancy,' she said. She went back to counting her money. She heard a footstep on the pavement behind her, and someone take a drag of a cigarette. It had to be Pete, but she didn't turn to check. She didn't want him or this American – what had he said his name was? Norman – thinking she needed any help.

Eventually, Norman seemed to realize she wasn't going to let him pull her. 'You open?' he asked Pete.

'Go right in,' said Pete in his irritating Australian accent. Norman pushed between him and Donna. At least he kept his hands to himself as he went.

Donna finished counting her money and shoved it in her purse. Pete was hovering at her right shoulder. He seemed to expect her to say something, so she glanced back at Norman and said, 'Hair of the dog?'

'After what he put away last night, he's gonna need the whole ruddy Rottweiler.'

Oh, very funny, Donna thought. She knew Pete expected her to laugh, but she couldn't be bothered. She just glanced at her watch and walked off. With a bit of luck she could get home, change, and still make the bus for the wives' lunch with the lads.

Hoo-bloody-ray for that, she thought. But there'd be hell to pay if she didn't go, and besides, it was better than knocking around the flat all afternoon on her own. She strode off down the street through the crowds of tourists, hardly bothering to look at the advertising banners that were strung across the road, or the shops with their garish displays of expensive imported Western goods and cheap knock-offs.

The bus-stop, she thought. Where is that bloody bus-stop? She found it eventually.

Fifteen minutes later, she was still standing there. Several buses had been past, but all of them had been the wrong numbers. Donna moved up to the head of the queue. There were a lot of people behind her, and she wondered if any of them wanted the same number she did. She'd have asked, but they'd only spout gibberish at her, she was certain. She looked at the timetable wired to the bus-stop, but she couldn't understand it – even the part written in English mentioned only places she'd never heard of. She slapped at it in disgust, sure now she would miss the bus and the wives' lunch and that Dave would be furious at her –

A hand gently touched her shoulder. She jumped. She turned. Mela, Joy's amah, was standing next to her. The Filipino woman smiled. 'Thank God for that,' Donna said. She pointed to the bus timetable. 'Is that the right one, then?' Mela smiled and nodded. Donna fumbled in her bag. 'D'you want a fag?'

'No, thank you.' She almost sounded disapproving, and Donna couldn't help noticing the way her hand went across her belly, as if protecting herself.

I shouldn't have told her, Donna thought. It was a bloody stupid thing to do. But she hadn't been able to help herself. It had been a couple of days earlier, when she'd realized she'd missed her second period. That and the way her breasts ached . . . anyway, she'd waited till Joy had gone to work, then nipped out and bought a pregnancy test. She'd stood there holding the swab under the tap, trying to pretend it hadn't gone blue.

But it had. So blue it was almost turquoise. So blue she'd wondered if she were carrying twins. Or, knowing her luck, quads. And Dave had been away at the border for ten days, and her mam was God knows how many thousand miles away in Newcastle, and Nancy was farting around with the SIB and even Joy was at work in the bloody crèche . . . and suddenly it was too much, and she was howling her head off. And then there'd been a gentle tap on the door, and Mela had been standing there. She couldn't speak

126

very good English, but she'd made Donna some of that jasmine tea muck, and got her to calm down, and eventually Donna had told her all about it. *Ma'am must think what she wants to do. Baby great joy if you want baby. If not – great sorrow*, she had said.

Well, Donna knew what she thought about the baby – and she didn't think it was a great joy.

'Ma'am is all right now?' Mela asked, cutting into Donna's thoughts. She sounded nervous.

'Do I bloody look all right?' Donna snapped. Bloody stupid question. 'Sodding eight weeks not all right, that's what I am.' Mela shot a nervous glance at the man behind Donna in the queue, as if she thought he could possibly have heard her over the rumble of traffic and the hooting of car horns. Well, Donna didn't bloody care who heard her. Let them all know. 'Eight weeks bloody gone,' she said again, louder, trying to make sure Mela understood. The other woman still said nothing. Donna took a long drag on her cigarette. It was supposed to be bad for your baby if you smoked when you were pregnant, but she didn't care. It wasn't really a baby, anyway. Just a blob, she thought. A little blob of jelly floating round inside me. Thinking anything else would drive her mad. 'I'm bloody terrified, if you must know,' she said in the end.

Mela was staring at her. She looked very young, standing there in the sunlight with those big brown eyes, but Joy had told Donna she had three kids of her own in the Philippines. 'If you like, ma'am – ' she began cautiously; but then she stopped and looked around, like a secret agent in a bad movie, making sure no one was listening. 'I will take you. Chinese lady – ' she turned, so that no one could see what she was doing except Donna. She looked up at her. 'She will – ' she hooked her finger and made a sharp pulling gesture. 'All done,' she said. She patted Donna gently on the arm. 'Good girl.'

Donna stared at her. An abortion? she thought. She's saying she can get me an abortion. For a moment it seemed like the answer to everything, and her only regret was that she'd told Dave. But that was okay – she could tell him she'd counted wrong, or that she'd lost it.

Mela said, 'All done – disco-disco?' She wiggled a bit, as if she were dancing, then spread her hands as if to say, Simple, you see, ma'am?

And Donna thought: an abortion. An illegal abortion, in the backstreets of Hong Kong. But it might be the best she could do.

Chapter 7

'Shit's gonna hit the fan for some poor sod, I reckon,' Paddy Garvey said.

Aye, Dave thought. Me. His patrol – Paddy, Dave, Tony Wilton and Jerry Foster – were standing at attention on the verandah outside Colonel Fortune's office. Dave knew they couldn't have been there more than five minutes, but he felt as if half his life had gone by while he stood there listening to the hushed voices from inside, and the squawking of parakeets in the jungle outside. But most of all he was listening to his own thoughts, to all the scuttlebut he'd heard that morning. Someone – he forgot who – had said that the Chief Superintendant of the Hong Kong Police had turned up. Tierney, that was his name. A real fire-breather, by all accounts. He'd reamed the old man out, and now the Colonel was ready to pass it on. So they said. Whoever *they* were.

Sweat trickled down Dave's back and down the bridge of his nose. There was a terrible itch just under his left eye, but he didn't dare move.

Not now, he thought. Not with the baby coming. Not when I wanted to make good.

'Looks like the old man's going to have a bloody canary,' Tony said, and then he screamed, 'Squad!'

Dave jerked to attention by reflex. He felt like peeing himself, but all he could do was stand there, facing front, shoulders back, belly in. Eyes level. His eyes would give him away, he knew that, so he forced himself to stare straight ahead, petrified the whole time that the Colonel would come and talk directly to him, because he really didn't think he could meet the old man's gaze.

He was in luck. The Colonel stood by the door. He stuck his hand on his hip and said quietly, 'Right. Cast your minds back to this morning's little pantomime.' It would have been easier if he'd yelled, Dave thought. Easier if he didn't have that magnetic presence that demanded you make the best of yourself. He forced himself to keep his eyes on the patch of wood directly ahead of him as the Colonel continued, 'Ask yourself if there's anything you forgot to tell us. Keep it quiet and you'll all be in deep, deep shit.' He paused. Looked at them all for a long moment. Just when Dave thought he would have to come clean, the Colonel said, 'Sergeant Wilton, we'll start with you.'

Dave could swear he heard Tony swallow. In his peripheral vision, he saw the two men go inside. The door thumped shut. No one spoke. Dave didn't move, but still in his peripheral vision he saw Paddy lean forward ever so slightly and look at him.

It was obvious, wasn't it? Something got fouled up, it would have to be down to Dave the fuck-up Tucker.

Donna saw the bus waiting outside the married

quarters. Joy was standing outside it. She must have seen Donna, because she looked pointedly at her watch, flicked back her long brown hair and climbed aboard the bus. Donna, for her part, slowed her fast walk to a slow sashay. She wasn't going to give the wives the idea she was hurrying just for them.

Well, it wasn't her fault she was late, was it? First of all the bus had taken ages to come, and then it had gone all round the houses where she was sure it wasn't supposed to go, and the sun had just poured in at the window and given her a rotten pounding headache. So when she'd got home she'd had to have a little lie down, and then a shower – couldn't go visiting not looking her best, now could she? – and then she'd found out she didn't have any fags left, so she'd had to go and get some: she certainly wasn't going all that way without a smoke, no matter what the moaning minnies said about not smoking on the bus.

Still, she was here now, wasn't she? She was about to say as much when she got on the bus – give them her best and brightest smile, the one she knew could charm the birds down out of the trees. But as she stepped up she heard one of them say, 'Look at her – I know where my old man'll be looking.'

She paused on the top step to make sure they all got a good eyeful of her – low cut mini-dress, high heels and all. Let those dowdy old baggages talk, she thought. Let 'em.

'Come on, Donna,' Joy said. 'We've been waiting ages.'

'It's only just gone twelve,' Donna snapped, knowing it wasn't true.

'Quarter past,' said the woman sitting behind Joy, waving her wrist in the air.

Donna didn't even know the old bat's name. She only looked to be in her twenties, but Donna reckoned she'd be in the Knitting Club and the Mother and Baby Club, and probably, God help her, the Sewing the Men's Badges On Club. She gave her a long hard look and said, 'Yeah, well you can't trust those cheap watches.'

She plonked herself down into a window seat, next to Mrs Fortune. Let the old slags eat that up, she thought. They'd be pea-green with envy, the small-minded little cows. She unfolded her sunglasses, which were hanging on a thong round her neck.

'How's it going, Donna?' Mrs Fortune asked.

Donna put the glasses on, feeling grateful that the mirrorshades would stop the other woman seeing her eyes. 'Great,' she said brightly, wishing she felt it.

Great, she thought. If you liked the Mother and Baby Club.

It was as bad as Dave had thought it would be. Colonel Fortune and Lieutenant Pereira didn't even bother to play good cop/bad cop. They just made him stand at attention in the baking heat of the office, while they fired the same questions at him over and over again.

Lieutenant Pereira moved round behind him. 'You were with the others all the time?'

It was all Dave could do to stop himself turning round. From somewhere outside came the constant chee-chee-cheeing of a jungle bird. It was getting right on Dave's nerves. 'Sir,' he said, wishing they'd let him stand a bit closer to the electric fan that whirred away in the corner.

Colonel Fortune paced back and forth, back and forth, then settled himself on the edge of his desk. 'Bloody miracles, my men.' He produced a handkerchief from his back pocket and mopped at his sopping forehead with it. 'All joined at the hip, charging off in opposite directions.'

Say nothing, Dave told himself. Never mind that he's been good to you – never mind that he's saved your arse more than once. Say nothing and they just can't get you.

'You were with the two suspects caught by the fishpond,' said Lieutenant Pereira from behind him. The man's voice was soft, almost gentle.

News to me, Dave thought. It must be something they'd got from Tony Wilton. He said nothing, knowing anything he did say might contradict what the Sergeant had said. Belly in, shoulders back, eyes front. That's all you have to think about, he told himself.

Then, suddenly, Colonel Fortune lost his patience. He slammed his hand down on the desk. 'If there's been a balls-up, tell me now.' He was speaking loudly, not yet shouting but letting Dave know he could if he wanted to. He stood up and spoke as he walked slowly over to Dave. 'With one court martial behind you, you can't afford to be anywhere near trouble.'

Dave winced, and wondered if the Colonel had spotted it. He'd been trying not to think about that — about the horrible time waiting for the court martial and then the long, grey days in military prison, all for a moment's anger.

Colonel Fortune came right up close and glared at him. 'Do you have anything to tell us?' The words were like machine-gun bullets.

'No, sir,' Dave said. He felt like his guts had turned runny, but he managed not to look away or blink. 'Don't know what you mean, sir.' He could hear Pereira's quiet breathing behind him. Someone else to let down.

The Colonel stared at him a moment longer. 'All right, Tucker,' he said. Then, to Dave's relief, he turned away, dabbing at the back of his neck with the handkerchief. He went back to his desk. 'We're here to do a job.' He leant across the desk, putting his weight on his arms, and now, for the first time, he shouted. 'And if anyone's deliberately fouling that up I'd like to be on the next plane out, because we're a total bloody embarrassment.'

Dave swallowed. He had to hold on, just for a few more seconds, that was all. The Colonel glared at him. He felt as if the officer's gaze could burn holes straight through him.

Colonel Fortune straightened up. He sat down. 'Right,' he said. 'Get out and send in Garvey before we're knee-deep in wives.'

Wives, Dave thought as he went out. Donna. Jesus. He'd all but forgotten her.

He went out and told Paddy to go in. He desperately wanted to tell him not to say anything, but he didn't dare. Then he went and joined the others, putting out the tables and chairs for the wives' lunch. All the time he worked – humping chairs from one place to another, then, like as not, humping them back again when padre Armstrong changed his mind, manhandling table-tops on to trestles and shaking out tablecloths – he said to himself, Paddy won't say anything because he can't; he didn't see anything so he won't say anything. Round and round the words went, but deep in his gut he knew that Paddy – or if not Paddy, then someone else – would blow the gaffe. If he'd dared he would have sneaked off for a quick can of Foster's, but he didn't dare, so all he could do was work.

And then the word went up that someone had seen the bus threading its way along the narrow path up the hillside. After that the men stood around, trying to act like the barbecue was nothing – the bunting, the crisp white tablecloths, the mountains of food – while every one of them watched the gate as if it might disappear if they took their eyes off it.

It rolled in. The men stopped talking. The doors opened.

One by one the wives got off the bus. Nancy, making no secret of how glad she was to see Paddy. Joy, refusing to go off with Tony because she wanted to make sure the others were okay, until he more or less dragged her off. Other women, the wives of men he hardly knew.

135

Dave wandered over to the bus. He stood facing the door, with his hands stuck in his pockets, waiting for her. So they'd talk about him. Well, they did that anyway, and none of it good.

He could see Donna sitting in the front seat, next to Mrs Fortune. The Colonel's wife was saying something to her, but she was staring out the window – not even the side facing him, but the one giving her an unrestricted view of the side of the Operations building. Finally, Mrs Fortune got up. She smiled at Tucker and for a horrible moment he thought she might be going to speak to him; but she didn't, she went off to talk to the padre instead.

A good five minutes later, Donna appeared at the top of the steps leading down from the bus. She was wearing a short dress so tight it could have been sprayed on, and with a plunge neckline that was just short of indecent. She rested against the door frame, with one hand on her shoulder-bag and the other clutching a closed paper fan.

One smile, he thought. Go on, pet. One smile'll make everything all right.

But she didn't smile, and suddenly he realized he was furious at her, and furious at the Chinese illegals, and furious at himself for screwing up yet again. 'Don't kill yourself rushing,' he said.

'Hello yourself,' Donna said. She stepped down off the bus, making her breasts bob under her dress, and giving Dave thoughts that ought to have been illegal in public.

'Thanks for coming, Donna,' she threw at him as

she walked straight past, slapping the bunting as she went.

Dave turned round slowly, not wanting to give her the satisfaction of thinking he was chasing her. She had stopped on the edge of the barbecue area. The dress, Dave decided, looked every bit as good from the back as it had from the front.

One smile, he thought. One sodding smile, that's all I wanted. He could hear his blood roaring in his ears, and knew if he wasn't careful he would lose his temper with her right in front of everyone. She'd never forgive him. He wasn't sure he cared.

'Is this it?' Donna said. She gestured contemptuously at the barbecue with her fan.

Yes this is it, Dave thought. Jungle and sweat and sun and more bloody jungle and that's all there is.

No, he thought. We aren't going to row. We might have to talk about – about the baby, but we aren't going to row. He went up to her, determined to be nice.

She turned round. 'Where's bloody China then?' she asked, but not as if she really wanted to know.

'There it is,' he said, gesturing past the bus, 'over there.' He went up to her, got close in so he could ask her the thing that had been on his mind since the morning – though it felt like he'd been thinking about it for most of his life. 'How's the baby?' She didn't answer him, didn't even turn to look at him. Stupid, Tucker, he thought at himself. She's not just a baby machine. 'Looking after yourself?' he re-phrased it.

'Well, there's no one else to look after me, is there?' she snapped.

'I get leave next weekend,' he said. Be pleased, he thought. Please be pleased.

'Do you?' It had at least got her attention. He moved in for a quick kiss, in case it was the only chance he got. She scowled and jerked away. 'Get off. You're just made up with being a dad.' She fiddled with the fan. 'It doesn't matter what I think, how I feel.'

'Look,' Dave said desperately, 'you'll get over it. It's a natural thing.' What could he say to help her feel happy with it? She ought to be happy with it, dammit. 'Paddy Garvey said –'

Before he could finish, Donna cut in. 'You told Paddy Garvey!' she shouted. She turned and stalked off, yelling, 'Thanks a lot,' as loud as she could.

Dave followed her, horribly aware that everyone – just everyone – was watching them. She halted by one of the tables and he caught up to her. 'Donna,' he whispered. He put his hand out to touch her shoulder, but didn't dare complete the action.

'We were supposed to be taking precautions,' she said. She was near tears. He wished they were alone, so he could help her – hold her, speak more freely, whatever it took. 'I'm bloody terrified, if you must know,' she said. 'Not that you care.'

All right, Dave thought. What would the padre say? Talk to her. Men, love your wives and do not be harsh with them. Big joke. He took a deep breath. Whatever happened, he wasn't going to lose his temper. 'All right,' he said. 'What are you terrified of?'

Donna looked at him as if he'd said the stupidest

thing in the world. 'Oh, aye! You can't even go to the dentist without being tied down, you!'

Well, fair enough, Dave thought. But there was anaesthetic, all kinds of injections they could give you . . .

He started to say as much, but she said, 'I'll tell you what, I'm not having it.' What? he thought. 'I'm getting rid of it,' she shouted. Before he could react, she was gone.

Dave chased her. 'You're bloody not,' he screamed, and this time he didn't care who heard.

She rounded on him. 'You watch us,' she snapped.

Suddenly, they were the centre of attention. 'I'll –' Dave started.

But just then the padre clapped his hands loudly from the back of the crowd. 'Scoffs on,' he shouted. 'Come and get it!'

Donna turned and stalked away, and once again Dave found himself pursuing her through the party. He caught up with her just as she grabbed an orange plastic chair, slammed it into position at the head of the table where the Garveys and Wiltons were sitting, and banged herself down into it.

Thought she could say what she liked and then get out of it by running off to friends, did she? Right. Well, he'd show her. 'You do that and I'll bloody kill you,' he yelled at her. It was all he could do to stop himself grabbing her, but he made do with shoving his finger in her face. She wouldn't look at him. 'I mean it!'

Paddy came round the table and tried to bundle

him away from her. 'Not here, mate,' he said. He put his hand on Dave's arm, and started to push him gently to the side, but just then the padre turned up.

'Everyone got full plates?' he asked brightly. Dave stared at him. It was obvious he really wanted to ask what was going on. And what the hell could Dave say, anyway?

Tony Wilton rescued him. 'Yeah, the steak was terrific, padre,' he said, twiddling a strip of it round on his fork.

The padre put a hand on Donna's shoulder. 'Everything all right, Donna?' he asked.

She looked up at him with a big smile plastered to her face. 'Yeah, lovely,' she said, but her voice was brittle.

The padre smiled at them all, nodded, and walked away. Paddy Garvey took a long swig out of his can of lager and sat down. Nancy smiled across at Joy, who reached out and squeezed Tony's hand.

Oh, they'd like to think everything was all right. They couldn't see past the next ten minutes, that was their problem. 'Just as long as 'wa plates are full,' Dave said to them, and smiled sourly. He leaned across the table, so there was no possibility that Donna could ignore him. 'Mine certainly is, you murdering bitch,' he said to her.

Donna leapt up pushing him back and sending the chair flying. She lashed out and slapped him hard across the face. It hurt. He doubled over with his hand to his cheek.

When he stood up, Donna had gone.

* * *

140

Later, when the wives had gone, he helped the others put the barbecue gear away. Some of the men were still buzzy from the afternoon, but a lot were a bit gloomy, knowing they weren't going to see the women again for a while.

Don't know how lucky they are, Dave thought as he stowed his load of bunting in one of the vans. He'd be seeing Donna next weekend, and what the hell would he say to her then? He turned round and started to go back for another load, then decided that he just couldn't be bothered and the consequences could go hang. He leant against the open back of the van, and started to swing the mesh door back and forth, back and forth as he wondered how they were ever going to get on with their lives after this. He knew he'd never forgive her if she got rid of it. A boy, it would have been – *would be*, he told himself fiercely. A right little tyke with a shock of black hair and big brown eyes like his mam. He'd teach him how to kick a ball, and when he was old enough he'd take him to the footie with him. It would be grand. Or if it were a girl, he'd have two beautiful women in his life. Just as long as the little darlin' got her mam's looks without her temper . . .

Just then Paddy came up with some more bunting, including the piece he was wearing draped round his neck. He pushed Dave out the way to put it in the van. Midnight was right behind him with the last of it. He had a cigarette stuck in his mouth, and the smoke from it wreathed around his face.

'Dave!' He said as he tossed the bunting into another van, then propped himself against the tailgate

141

and took the fag out of his mouth. 'What's this I hear?'

'What?' Dave snarled. Got clobbered by me wife, is that what you heard? Or maybe that she sat sulking on the bus half the afternoon?

'You gonna be a dad, then?' Midnight was grinning broadly.

'What if I am?' Dave demanded. Christ half the men in the Fusiliers must know by now.

'Nothing,' Rawlings said. 'Bloody hell – touchy!' He looked disgusted as he stood up, tossed his butt away and went off.

'You just mind your own bloody business,' Dave called after him. He rounded on Paddy. 'You going to announce the abortion as well?'

Paddy looked astonished. 'What?' he demanded.

Dave sighed and looked at the ground. Hadn't the soft sod worked it out after that little scene at the barbecue?

Paddy grabbed his shoulders and shook him. 'Dave,' he said, in a tone that said he thought Tucker was the soft one. 'This time tomorrow she'll be knitting romper suits and shovelling down kippers and marmalade. You'll see.'

'Not her,' Dave muttered. He still wanted to be left alone, but part of him – part of him wanted to say to anyone at all what he couldn't say to Donna. He looked across the car park. 'Nothing's like they make out, is it?' A couple of men walked by, carrying a table top between them. Jesus, he thought. I am soft. Bloody soft, Dave the screw-up Tucker. And not just

142

about Donna either. 'I made one hell of a cock-up this morning, Paddy.' The Corporal stared at him. He straightened up, glad of the chance to tell someone at last – to explain what he'd seen in that boy's eyes. 'Look – ' he began.

'If you're going to tell me what I think you are, don't.' He shoved Dave back against the van, but gently.

'Paddy – '

'I don't want to know.' Another pair of fusiliers went by with another table-top. Paddy dropped his voice to an urgent hiss. 'And if you had any bloody sense at all, you'd get it sorted.' He jabbed Dave in the chest, not gently at all this time. 'Now,' he finished.

He turned and walked away.

If I had any sense at all I probably would, Dave admitted to himself. But then, I haven't got any sense. After all, I'm just Dave the screw-up.

Nancy was a canny lass, Donna thought, feeling glad she'd sat next to her. At least she had the sense to keep quiet about the row. She stared out of the window, watching the dry tan earth unroll before the bus as they drove down the hill, while beyond it the mountains reared up behind the expanses of cleared and re-grown jungle. Jungle, she thought. What the hell am I doing here – me a townie born and bred, thought I was going into the wilds if I got further away from Newcastle city centre than Gateshead. Yet there it was when she looked out of the window:

143

dense green and lush, spiked with sudden slashes of crimson and sapphire as a parrot or some other nameless bird darted overhead.

Well, she'd known what it would be when she married him. She couldn't really claim she hadn't known. Her head felt as if it were going to explode. She had to talk to someone. Nancy was as good as anyone else.

'What am I going to do, Nance?' she asked, knowing the other woman would understand. 'I just can't have this kid. I can't.'

Nancy grinned at her sympathetically. 'You aren't the first woman in the world to get upset because you're pregnant, you know. It's hardly a crime.'

Donna pouted in disgust. 'You try telling him that.' What had he called it? A natural thing? Well, so was dying and she wasn't planning on doing that any time soon, either. 'What I need –' she started, then stopped as she tried to figure out the best way to put it. 'What I need is a plan – so I can tell him, like, this is how it's going to be, and you can like it or lump it.' He'd come round then, she was sure of it. After all, it wasn't him that was going to get lumbered with the kid, and it wasn't him that was going to lie there screaming in agony as they yanked it out of him. The very thought set her teeth on edge.

Nancy looked at her dubiously. 'Well,' she said after a moment, 'There's a family planning place in Stanley. You wouldn't have to worry about the army doctor then.'

That simple? Donna thought. All this bloody

worry and it's that simple? I needn't even have bothered telling him. 'Would they do it?'

'Well, they'd talk to you about it.' Nancy hooked her leg up on to the seat and clasped her hands round her knee.

'Oh, I can't talk about it, man,' Donna said. Not to some stuck-up middle-class old bag who'd lecture her on contraception and God knew what else. They'd ask her why she wanted to get rid of it, and what could she say? That she wanted to disco-disco every night, like Mela said? Or the truth, which was that she was scared to death of the pain? She sighed, trying to find the words to explain. 'I just can't. It makes me feel sick. I've always been the same. Dave didn't want kids, either.' They'd had their problems – didn't everyone? – but she'd always thought they felt the same about most things – work a bit, play hard, and suffer the consequences when you couldn't get out of it. Until now. She felt let down by him: him and his wanting to be a dad, as if he knew what being a dad was all about. Betrayed, that's the word for how I feel. Well, two could play at that game. 'I just want it out, now – before it's too late.'

Nancy thought for a second. 'Well, there's a swanky clinic in the Peak. No questions asked, but it is pricey.'

Silly cow, Donna thought. 'If I had money I'd go home, wouldn't I?' she snapped. Stupid bloody woman, she thought at Nancy – getting my hopes up like that. She flipped her fan open, and wafted it in front of her face. 'All on me own,' she muttered to herself, but loud enough so she could be sure Nancy heard it. 'As sodding usual.'

It should have been the perfect end to a perfect day – out of uniform and into shorts and not a lot else, sitting round with the lads talking about the barbecue and downing a few ice-cold cans while the sun went down. But Dave didn't feel like joining in. What was the point? It would only spoil their fun, considering that the main topics of conversation were bound to be the row he'd had with Donna, Donna whacking him one, and the screw-up with the escaping illegals that morning. And that would be really hard to sit and listen to, at least without giving himself away. So he ended up kicking around the camp looking for anything he could do to make himself look busy – even work. But no matter what he did, he couldn't help noticing the other blokes looking at him, and whispering as he went by. It felt like that, anyway.

Might be easier to go and sit down, he decided in the end. They'd shut up if he did that. He ambled across to one group, then thought better of it. Midnight, Paddy and some of the others were sitting across the way, playing cards. He wandered that way, with his hands in the pockets of his shorts, trying to look like he hadn't got a thing to worry about. Midnight looked at his hand, then glanced up. He caught Dave's eye, then looked away. 'Nice seeing the girls, eh lads?' he said round his mouthful of gum. 'For some of us anyway.' He sniggered.

Let it go, Dave thought. Just let it bloody go, him

and his stupid neckerchief and his baseball cap and his stinking chewing-gum – he's not worth getting into grief for. He walked past, trying to look like he'd never meant to join them; but the muscles of his back and neck were rigid with tension, and he felt his hands ball up into fists in his pockets.

From behind him, Dave heard Paddy say, 'Give it a rest, will you?'

Thanks, mate, he thought.

But Midnight went on, 'Well, his wife gives him grief and the whole bleedin' platoon grinds to a halt.' Dave paused. He took a deep breath. Blood roared in his ears. Midnight said, 'Bet it was him who landed him in it with the old man and all.' Dave was next to Midnight's chair before he even realized he was moving. He felt his lips peel back and his breath come in hard little pants, but there was nothing in the world except his blazing anger. 'Extra sodding patrols –' Midnight said, just as Dave hauled him out of his seat.

He grabbed the neckerchief Midnight was wearing. 'What do you know about my wife,' he yelled.

Midnight's hand slapped into his chest, and he stumbled back a couple of steps. 'The same as everyone else does,' he said. He glared at Dave, who glared right back.

Before either of them could do anything, Paddy leapt out of his seat and knocked Midnight out of the way. He pushed Dave back. 'He's all mouth, Dave. He doesn't know sod all.' Tucker tried to barge past Paddy, but the Corporal used his greater bulk to block him. 'Just leave it.'

Dave made another lunge at Midnight, and again Garvey grabbed him. 'Don't tell me, Paddy,' he snarled, pointing at himself. He made one last try. 'Tell him to shut his mouth,' he screamed, jabbing his finger at Midnight.

Paddy knocked his arm down, then angled round so that he was completely between the two men. He jabbed his finger into Dave's chest. 'No, I'm telling you.' His face was pink with anger. 'You want to be a dad? You want to try growing up first.'

Dave glared at him. He's your mate, he told himself. Midnight's your mate. You don't want to be fighting with your mates when you'll need all the friends you can get. But the roaring in his ears wouldn't go away, and he could still feel his heart thumping in his chest. He took a couple of long, deep breaths. 'Yeah,' he said sourly. 'Well, it doesn't matter now, because it's not going to happen, is it?'

He shook Paddy's hand off and walked away.

Slowly, the anger subsided. He should go back, crack a can and a joke if he could think of one – which was a laugh in itself, when his whole bloody life felt like one big joke – and let their snide remarks wash over him. They'd stop soon enough when they got bored, which they would soon enough if he didn't react.

But he couldn't do it. Everywhere he looked he saw Donna's face, heard her saying, *I'm bloody terrified, if you must know*. But he hadn't known, and he wasn't sure if it made any difference. He'd never wanted a kid before, but only because he'd never really thought he could have one. As soon as she'd said she was pregnant – he hadn't even realized she was late – he'd known that being a dad was what he wanted. More than anything, he thought. Maybe even more than Donna, and he hadn't thought that was possible.

It was too much to think about. But every time he tried to let go of it, he started seeing the two Chinese intruders he'd let go. Christ, the kid couldn't have been more than five. They'd smelled of something lemony, and of sweat. He thought, if that was my kid – if I had a kid and he got into trouble – I'd want someone to give him a chance. When it happened, he hadn't been able to put it in words, but he could now.

That was all he had done. Given them a chance.

He went into the barracks and slowly changed out of his shorts and into his camo uniform, ready for the evening patrol. By the time he was ready, the others were starting to come into the room, Midnight among them.

He stared as if he were going to say something, but Dave just pushed past him and went outside. He still had a good hour to kill, and he didn't know how to get through it. He felt a terrible restlessness, an urge to go somewhere, do something – maybe hit someone. Anything but stand around looking at the camp buildings for another second.

He did the only thing he could think of – he walked down to the perimeter fence. He looked at it for a minute. It reminded him more than anything of a fence round a school playground. But what was out there was more dangerous than any main road, any stranger offering sweeties. What was out there could wreck his life. Two illegal immigrants, one a kid and the other with a wounded leg, out there in the jungle somewhere. He went right up close to the fence and stood with his hands clenched round the chain link and his face pressed up close, staring out at the impenetrable mass of green that was the jungle, willing them to appear.

But if they did, he didn't know what he would do about it.

'Getting the cold shoulder treatment?'

The voice came from behind him. He turned and saw padre Armstrong at his shoulder. 'No, padre,' he lied.

'Is this the way to get that first stripe?' The padre's voice was kind but insistent, strong from years of giving sermons rather than bawling at men on the parade ground.

It was enough – almost enough – to make Dave weep. 'That doesn't matter any more.' He sighed. Nothing much mattered any more. The chain-link fence seemed like a prison to him. Well, he'd better get used to it. It was probably where he was going to end up, after this morning. He forced away memories of his other spell in prison. He'd sworn then it would never happen again, but he suddenly knew deep in his belly that he'd been wrong: what he'd done that morning was sure to be found out. He sighed, then sighed again, remembering he was supposed to be talking about Donna. 'She doesn't want the baby.' He felt the wire bite into his fingers. 'I don't know what she wants.'

'Dave, give her a chance — '

Even the sodding padre sounded fed up with him. Suddenly it was too hard to think about Donna and the baby son who wasn't going to grow up to kick a ball around in the garden and go to footie matches with him; and that only left the two Chinese illegals, but all he'd done was to try and give them a chance when they had nothing, the way the poor little baby inside Donna should be given a chance. He whirled round, off the fence. 'I didn't take any money,' he said. He stared at Armstrong, who looked back with an expression of complete bewilderment on his face. Dave realized the man didn't have any idea what he was talking about. 'They were kids,' he said, and realized to his horror that he was almost weeping. 'Bloody soldiers chasing after bloody kids,' he shouted. He turned back and grabbed the fence again, trying to find some sense in the dark green of the jungle. But there was no sense in anything. 'They looked terrified.'

'You'll have to tell the Old Man,' the padre said.

'Yeah,' Dave muttered, so quietly he could hardly hear it himself. But he wasn't ready to face that yet. He took a long ragged breath and turned back to face into the camp. He leaned back against the fence, but he couldn't make himself face the padre. 'Oh, I thought if they got a few miles away they'd be okay — down into Central sweeping the streets.' He glanced at the padre. 'Better than prison.' He couldn't hold the man's gaze. He looked at the ground.

'They wouldn't have been sent to prison, you clown.' The padre sounded amused. Yep, Dave thought. That's me. Tucker the screw-up, Tucker the clown, Tucker the butt of every joke going. 'All right,' the padre said, suddenly all business. 'Just tell the Old Man you lost them.' He stared hard at Dave. 'Don't try to be funny. He isn't in the mood.'

Dave had never felt less like being funny in his life.

He followed the padre down to Colonel Fortune's office, then had to wait for an agonizing few minutes – that felt more like hours – outside, while the two men talked.

Eventually, he was called inside. He came to attention as smartly as he could, given that he was almost shaking.

'I found them, sir. They'd got separated from the others,' he said. He wondered what he could say that wouldn't trip him up later, or contradict what they already knew. 'One of them was injured. The other one – ' he felt the panic boiling up in him again when he thought of the kid, but he bit it back down. He was beginning to understand that it was linked up with Donna's pregnancy, and the way he wanted her to have the baby. 'He was just a kid. A nipper – I don't suppose they could keep up. The others – ' he paused. This was the tricky bit. 'They were trying to get the other illegals under control – ' he licked his lips. He didn't want to tell a direct lie, but at least he already knew the others had said they all stayed together.

'And you went off to help them, leaving the two

you'd found alone,' Colonel Fortune supplied for him.

'Yes, sir,' Tucker said. He glanced at the padre, but the man's face might have been carved from marble for all the expression it showed.

'Without securing them?'

'There wasn't time, sir.' Just keep looking straight ahead, Dave told himself. Never mind about meeting his eyes, just keep looking at that spot on the wall where the clock used to be.

The Colonel walked over to the window. He stared out of it for a long time, with his hands clasped behind his back. He was a bull of a man, with a powerful build and a face that looked as if it had been roughly carved out of a lump of granite. He wasn't a man you wanted to have angry with you, Dave thought; but angry was what he was – it was obvious from the way he was standing, and in his quiet, clipped tones.

Dave had known him a long time, and he knew that what really rankled with the Colonel was the fact that Dave had lied to him. Well, he was still lying. The Old Man had just better not find out about it, that was all.

He turned and strode over to Dave. 'Because the padre's a Christian,' he said, 'And because I'm getting soft, let's say you always intended to go back and get them.' He crossed his arms, making himself seem even broader than before.

'I think that's true,' the padre said, and added, 'isn't it, Tucker?' in a tone that said Dave would be a bloody fool to deny it.

153

'Of course it is,' Colonel Fortune said, and Dave thought: he knows, but he's giving me a chance . . . it was more than he deserved and far more than he'd hoped for. He realized, with a shock, that there was the shadow – not even that, the ghost of a shadow – of a smile on the Colonel's lips.

Dave felt suddenly light-headed. 'I did, sir, but –' he swallowed. A chance! They thought enough of him to give him a second chance, no questions asked. ' – they were gone, sir.' He didn't dare catch the eye of either man. 'Sorry, sir.'

'Go on,' the Colonel said. 'Get ready for the night patrol.' Dave saluted, then headed for the door. 'Oh and Tucker?' said the Colonel from behind him. He turned. 'For God's sake don't do anything like that again – I'm running out of excuses, understand me.'

'Yes sir,' Dave said.

Night patrol, he thought. The others were going to love that.

Chapter 8

The camp by night was just as hot, just as sticky, and just as interesting – which was to say, not very – as the camp by day. The platoon was mustered on the parade ground, waiting to move out in the trucks and begin their patrols.

Midnight's right, Dave thought. This is all my fault. But that was okay. He'd find the two illegals and this time he'd bring them in. What had the padre told him as they walked down to the Colonel's office? That they wouldn't be sent to prison, but just given two weeks' re-education, whatever that was.

He tried to pay attention to what Colonel Fortune was saying – or, rather, shouting. He strode up and down the line as he spoke: 'Dogs are on standby and so is the helicopter. If you need Nite Sun, radio. It'll be with you in minutes.'

Dogs, Dave thought. Helicopters. Nite Sun – just what they needed: terrify the poor bastards with bright lights and overkill. Anyone would think they were a couple of serial killers on the loose, rather than a slip of a lad younger than Dave was and a kid not old enough to be in school. And that was without considering that the older one was injured. A wound like that would be festering by now. You'd get flies in it. Maggots, maybe. And it would hurt like hell.

Colonel Fortune reached the end of the line and turned back, lit only by the pale light of the moon and the glare of the trucks' headlamps. 'This isn't a pair of kids we're dealing with,' he said. Yes it bloody is, Dave thought. And you know it too. 'It's two illegal immigrants who were seen by one of us and allowed to escape.' The Old Man's gaze rested on Dave just for a second. Mentioning no names, of course, Dave thought. Thank you very much, sir. The Colonel continued, 'This just never happens. Never.'

Yeah, Dave thought. But the army border patrol never had Dave the Screw-up on their side before, did they.

Colonel Fortune came to a halt front and centre. If he'd been shouting before, now he thundered. 'If you see anything, you make your report there and then, and we act immediately – not twelve hours later.' Midnight turned his head just enough so that he could look at Dave. His expression was one of disgust. 'All right, Rawlings, you can spare us the righteous indignation.' Midnight looked away sharply enough, but he'd made his point. 'That's my job,' the Old Man said. 'You just get out there and do yours.'

Yeah, Dave thought, as they were dismissed. It had seemed so simple before he'd listened to the Colonel: he was going to make the best of the second chance he'd been given, and that was that. But the more the Old Man talked about them being illegal immigrants and not just kids, the more he saw the little 'un's big brown eyes staring up at him.

Re-education, he told himself firmly. That's what they'd get, not prison.

Sounded like brainwashing to him.

Donna followed Mela from the waterfront to the main tourist drag, where she pushed her way through crowds of people, their faces painted garish colours by the kaleidoscope of flashing neon lights. The noise from the clubs and bars was too loud — hammer-blows of rock and jazz and reggae all slamming to-gether — and she was far too hot. She felt light-headed: she'd picked at a cheese sandwich at teatime, and then only because she thought she ought to eat. Anyway, she wished she hadn't even eaten that much — her stomach was churning that badly.

Mela turned a corner. The lights were smaller here, and there were girls lining the street. They glared at her as if she were an invading army all by herself. A couple of men stood in a doorway, watching her.

Christ, she thought. Red-light district. Mela walked even faster. A man — a Westerner — walked up to Mela, but saw Donna before he spoke to her. He started to come up to her, but one of the street walk-ers cut in. Mela looked back, paused for Donna to catch up, then turned a corner. She went through an unmarked door with peeling paint. Donna went in too, and waited while Mela talked to the doorman in rapid Chinese.

Then she turned to Donna, and pointed to some stairs at the end of the hallway, where an old Chinese woman sat. Donna licked her lips and pulled at the flap of her washed-denim jacket. Mela started towards the stairs, and there was nothing for Donna to do but follow.

Dave's patrol eased their way through jungle turned ghostly by the moonlight. In the dead quiet of the night every breaking twig sounded like a gunshot, every rustle of grass like an approaching predator. Tony led them across a grassy clearing to a patch of dense jungle. Motioning for them to crouch down, he peered into it.

A torch, Dave thought. I'd give my right flaming arm for a torch.

Donna stared past Mela and the old woman, who were chattering in Chinese, to the smoke-filled room beyond, where old men were sitting round sipping cups of tea or spirits while they clacked down mah-jong tiles and barked bets at each other. The air was blue with incense and tobacco smoke, and heavy with the stink of curry and body odour and cheap perfume all mixed up together. A couple of Chinese girls – hookers by the look of them – took drinks around on trays, and plates of noodles and snacks.

They're looking at me, Donna thought. They know! She pulled her bag across her tummy. It can't show yet, she thought. I'm only eight weeks –

The old woman tapped her arm, then led her on – thankfully, not through the room but across the end of it, to another set of stairs. Donna looked back at Mela, who smiled encouragingly.

Just me on my sodding own again then, Donna thought. It didn't surprise her.

Dave heard something – a rattling in the bushes. He clicked his fingers once and then more urgently, to get Tony's attention. The sergeant turned in a low crouch and Dave pointed. A duck flew straight at Dave. He bit back a bellow and stumbled back, slashing at it with his baton. The bird fell to the ground, fluttered once and was still.

The old woman led Donna up the stairs, then up again, and once more. She turned to Donna and said something unintelligible. Donna just stared at her. Then they came out into a small room, where a man was counting long yellow incense sticks from a jar into his hand. A light, filtered through a curtain of glass beads, came from a room beyond. The old woman pushed Donna gently in that direction, and then again, harder. There was nothing for her to do but go through.

The bush behind Dave rattled. Another bloody duck, he thought, remembering the grin on Paddy's face. But it didn't sound like a duck, or a fox either, come to that. He raised his hand and started to click his fingers, but then thought better of it.

The bush rattled again. He turned and peered into the shadows. Something was moving in there, black on black, too big to be an animal.

Stay together. Tony had warned him.

To hell with it.

He hefted his baton, then turned and pushed his way between the overhanging branches. Something white was moving in there.

He saw them at the same time as they saw him. The older lad raised his hand. Moonlight flashed on dull metal.

A gun. Dave registered it and had his hands in the air in the same heartbeat. Where the hell had they got it – if he'd known ... but it was far too late for maybes and might-have-beens.

The two illegals stared at him for a long moment. The older lad's leg was drenched with blood and tied roughly with a rag. The younger one, standing by his side, said something scared-sounding in Chinese. He was pale and Dave could almost see him shaking with exhaustion.

The gun wavered in the older lad's hand. He won't shoot, Dave thought. I ought to yell out for the others. But he didn't dare.

The next instant, the lad said something gutteral in Chinese. He backed off, one step, two. Then he turned and fled, hauling the little lad with him.

Dave stared at the place where they had been for a second. Then he threw back his head and howled in fury. All the anger, all the fear and disappointment and outrage at Donna came pouring out of him in that one long scream.

Then he charged off after them.

Donna sidled into the room. It was lit by a bare

160

overhead bulb, and a floor-standing spotlight made of rusty white metal. She noticed in passing that there were cardboard boxes stacked all around, but the main item of furniture was an old hospital trolley covered in a grubby white sheet. There was a stand next to it, with bottles and jars and an enamel tray. On a soiled pad inside it there were surgeon's instruments. Donna recognized a couple of speculums, forceps, a clamp, a couple of pairs of tweezers. She couldn't see anywhere to wash them in the room, let alone sterilize them.

A woman came through the far door. She was dressed in an ordinary blue tunic and top, and though her long hair was up, it was uncovered. She barked something in Chinese. Donna stared at her, then back at the instruments.

Instruments? she thought. Instruments of torture, more like. What if I bleed? If I haemorrhage? Christ, what about AIDS? Or that other thing – hepatitis?

And if not that, she suddenly had a vision of herself lying on the trolley with her legs spread wide while the woman fumbled around inside her, while she screamed in agony and had to be held down by some of those disgusting old men outside.

And if the abortion didn't kill her, Dave would anyway.

The woman glared at her impatiently. She gestured at the table, and said something harsh.

Donna stared at her for a second. Then she wheeled round and pushed through the bead curtain. She barrelled between the two hookers who were standing at the top of the stairs. One of them screamed abuse at her as she went past, but she didn't stop. She clattered down the stairs three at a time. Her hand, slick with sweat, skidded on the banister rail. The breath jolted out of her with each step as she went down and down until at last she reached the bottom. She fled past the old men, who stopped playing mah jong to stare at her. Behind her, the clicking of the tiles started up again, and over it a buzz of excited conversation. She raced down the hallway, grabbed Mela by the hand, hauled the door open and charged through.

She heard it slam behind her, but she didn't dare stop. She raced through the neon night, and they were halfway back to the waterfront before she realized they weren't being followed.

Dave pounded through the jungle, slashing at ferns and overhanging branches with his baton. He could hear them crashing around ahead of him, and behind him the rest of his patrol in pursuit. His heart hammered in his chest. He breathed deep and hard, and forced a bit of extra speed out of his pistoning legs.

They burst out of the jungle into an area of long grass. The rest of the platoon were nearly up with Dave now, spread out in a line and beginning to circle.

He heard a dog yowl some way off – further in front of him than the illegals – and knew that Paddy must have radioed in. That meant that the chopper and Nite Sun wouldn't be far behind. He had to get to them first. Had to. One more effort –

Too late. The dog-handler closed in from the far side of the clearing. The illegals hesitated, then came to a halt. The older one screamed and pulled out his gun. The dog yapped and snarled, and somewhere off to the side Tony Wilton shouted something. The chopper chup-chup-chupped almost at the limit of hearing.

The illegal's face, smeared with blood and sweat and grime, glistened darkly in the moonlight. He shouted something again.

Dave dropped his baton and put his hands out. He took a tentative pace forward. 'Don't do that,' he said quietly, not sure if the man could understand him. In answer, the illegal jabbed the gun at him.

Impasse.

But only for a couple of seconds. Then the whole clearing was lit in the glare of Nite Sun as the helicopter clattered overhead. The illegal squinted up at it. Dave thought about jumping him, but he was waving the gun around more or less in the direction of Paddy Garvey. The younger kid, forgotten, staggered a step or two away.

Foster grabbed him. He screamed and kicked and reached for the older illegal, who also started to bellow. Fear came off him like the stink of sweat as he thrust the gun out ahead of him. Any minute now, he was going to do something really stupid.

'The kid!' Dave yelled over the chuddering of the chopper and the illegal's shouting. 'Give him the kid back – ' and then, quietly to the illegal: 'It's all right, no one's going to hurt you – ' He put his hands out towards the man.

The dog leapt and snarled on its chain. 'Go the dog now – ' Tony Wilton screamed.

'No!' Dave shouted.

'Now!' Wilton ordered. 'Now! NOW!'

The dog-handler loosed the animal. It leapt straight at the illegal and locked its jaws round his gun hand. The man crashed to the ground screaming in terror. Dave lunged forward. The dog was standing at bay over the man, still with its teeth in his arm. Dave yanked the dog by the scruff of its neck. It wouldn't let go. Without thinking, Dave tried to force its jaws open. It snapped at him. He felt its teeth connect with his hand, and saw blood trickle across his skin. It was only then that he felt the pain lance through his hand and up into his arm.

The dog-handler came and pulled the dog off. Dave stood up clutching his hand. It had gone numb, and his skin was slicked with blood. Paddy grabbed the illegal while Tony retrieved the gun. The little Chinese lad was still screaming, still staring at them with terrified eyes.

'They're kids,' Dave yelled, 'only kids.' He felt as if he would explode with frustration and rage.

'Dangerous bloody kids,' Tony shouted back, thrusting the gun butt-first towards Dave. He waved to the chopper and the Nite Sun winked out.

Thoughts tumbled through Dave's brain – the weapon, re-education – no prison for sure, at least for the older one – the kid and Donna and the abortion she'd have whether he wanted it or not – and before he knew what he was doing he'd launched himself at

Tony. He grabbed the gun before the Sergeant could react, and hurled it at the water. There was a splash as it broke the water.

Dave turned to Tony. 'Aye,' he said. 'Well, they're not dangerous now,' he said. Tony glared at him. A muscle jumped beneath his eye. 'And I didn't see any gun. Did you?' Dave demanded.

No one said anything. In the distance there was the rumble of the approaching pick-up vehicle.

Trouble? Dave thought. I haven't known what trouble is, compared with this.

Chapter 9

The trouble with karaoke bars was that you had to put up with whoever was singing. Even if they couldn't sing. Even if they insisted on singing 'The Green Green Grass of Home', when what you wanted most in all the world was your mam.

Donna leant up against the optics bar and sniffled into her handkerchief. She just couldn't make herself stop crying. She wanted Newcastle and she wanted her mam, but she was stuck with the Jouster Inn, and the bloody karaoke singer, and – worst of all – the baby growing inside her.

Pete Lewis, the bar manager, brought a tray of dirty glasses round the back of the bar. He bumped her with them to get her to move, then set them down by the washer. She should have been doing that, but she didn't care. At least he'd given over nagging her about it for a while.

She glanced up. Mike was talking to the irritating Yank who'd been hanging around her ever since she'd started working there. He looked at her, said something to Mike and then strolled round the bar. She'd have to serve him; there was no way out of it. She smoothed down the stupid Union Jack overall Pete made her wear and stepped up to the bar. She hoped her mascara wasn't smudged. On second thoughts, she didn't care – let the smarmy bastard think what he liked.

'That's what I miss,' he said. He jerked his thumb at the stage, where the would-be Tom Jones was groaning out the last few lines of the song.

'Grass?' Donna said sceptically. As a chat-up line, it lacked a bit.

'Home,' the Yank said as if she were stupid. 'And grass. The pool. The prairie – '

Tell us another one, Donna thought. 'In New York?' Just for a second she was prepared to believe him – anything to distract her from the memory of that upstairs room, with its grubby trolley and the dirty instruments in their dirty bowl.

He didn't even have the good grace to look embarrassed. 'Up-state New York,' he said smoothly.

Typical lying bloody male, Donna thought. 'Piss off, you poser,' she snapped and stalked off. She slammed a glass up to an optic – double vodka.

Mike Lewis glared at her. She wasn't supposed to drink on duty. Well tough bloody luck, she thought. If he didn't like it he could take it out of her wages, and if that wasn't good enough then he could stuff his rotten job.

The locker room was hot and steamy. Dave propped himself up against the wire mesh partition that separated the lockers from the shower area. He was standing there because he wanted to talk to Paddy, and Paddy had been told to guard the prisoners. He winced as the medic pulled his arm round,

167

then winced again as the man swabbed the wound with antiseptic. He felt hollow, as if the shower he'd taken had not only eased his aching muscles but also washed away his ability to worry.

Not that he didn't have plenty to worry about.

On the other side of the room the older of the two illegals was showering with his back to them. The kid was watching him – the man had insisted on getting him cleaned up first.

And Paddy watched both of them, as if they were likely to do a runner.

The door banged open, and Tony Wilton came in with a tray of tea. Three mugs. The medic was on duty and the illegals obviously didn't rate any. Tony must have noticed Dave counting. 'They're doing them some grub,' he said.

He glanced at the two Chinese. There was something about the way the kid looked at the older lad that got right to Dave – as if he thought the older illegal could solve any problem the world could throw at them . . . the way a son might look at his father. Not that Dave was ever going to find out for himself. 'Poor little sods,' he said.

'Poor little sods!' Tony repeated, incredulous. 'He nearly blew your head off, Dave.' He picked up two of the mugs and brought them round. 'I'll have to tell 'em,' he muttered when he got close enough that the medic could at least pretend not to have heard.

'Yeah, I know,' Dave said. Friendship only went so far, after all. Tony, when all was said and done, was a Sergeant and the only wonder of it was they'd managed to stay this close. Especially with Dave having the reputation he did for screwing up. It just proved what a good mate Tony Wilton was – any other Sergeant would have done his best to get Dave shipped out of his platoon.

And Paddy – well, Paddy was on his way up, that was for sure. So it was a bit astonishing when he said, 'Why?'

'Why?' Tony repeated.

'Look at the poor bastard,' Paddy said, glancing over at the illegal, who was just about done with the shower. 'Don't you think he's got enough problems? And Dave, for that matter.'

Tony slammed the mug down on the table hard enough to make the tea slop everywhere. He stalked away, then turned. He looked as if he might be going to say something, but just at that moment Lieutenant Pereira came in.

'Right,' he said before even Tony could come to attention. 'Get them processed and stick them in detention.'

The older illegal was out of the shower. Paddy chucked him a towel. He caught it awkwardly because he was trying to keep his back turned to them, and started patting himself dry with it. It was far too small for the job, even though he wasn't much more than skin draped over bone. He glanced at them quickly with flat, unreadable eyes, then looked away.

'He won't top himself, will he, sir?' Dave asked Pereira. 'Death before dishonour and all that –'

'That's the Japanese, you prat,' Paddy said.

'Well, it's the same thing, isn't it?' Dave looked

with interest at the way the medic was bandaging his hand. It was going to be quite impressive when it was finished.

'Sir,' Tony said. Then he stopped. He opened his mouth as if he were going to say something more. Go on then, Dave thought. I won't hold it against you. But next to him he could sense, rather than see, Paddy glaring at the Sergeant. Tony closed his mouth again. Then he said, 'What happens to them next, sir?' just as if that was what he intended to say all along.

Lieutenant Pereira shrugged. 'Send them back.' The older illegal had put on the shorts they'd provided him with, and he was hugging the little boy to him. Pereira grinned. 'Well, they didn't exactly put up a fight, did they?' That's our Mr Paella, Dave thought. Right on the button as usual. 'Debrief in five minutes,' Pereira said. He turned and left.

When the sound of his boots clattering on the ceramic tiles had died away, Dave turned to the Sergeant. 'Thanks, Tony,' he said. 'You're a good mate.'

Tony glared at him for a minute. 'I don't think you understand the system, Tucker,' he said. He walked towards Dave. 'I'm not supposed to be your sodding mate.' He shoved his face right up close to Dave's. There were two patches of colour high on his cheekbones, and the tendons in his neck stood out like cords. 'I'm supposed to be your sodding Sergeant.' He held Dave's gaze for a long, painful moment. Then he stalked off.

There was silence. Then Paddy leant down to Dave and said, 'He won't say anything.'

Dave wasn't so sure. But he'd done what he'd done and there was no turning back from it. 'Well, whatever happens, I'm not sorry,' he said.

For a moment he even believed it.

Donna was really letting rip. After a certain point the only way to deal with a karaoke bar was to get up there yourself and show them how it was done. Besides, she liked the feeling of being looked at: just for once it made her feel important, as if she mattered in the world. Even if one of the men doing the looking was the American creep, *and* he insisted on joining in. Out of tune, too.

Given her mood, she was singing the only song that made any sense to her: 'Stand By Your Man'.

Mind you, she wasn't sure if she was belting it out to let the world know what she intended to do or to try and convince herself of what she ought to do.

It didn't matter. Not with the audience joining in the choruses and the men letting her know what they thought of her looks. Even if she was pregnant.

Pete came over. 'Oy! Dolly Parton!' He grabbed the microphone and flicked the switch on the karaoke machine. The audience shouted a protest.

'Hey, I was enjoying that,' yelled the American; so he was good for something then.

'Get back behind that bar,' Pete said. 'I'm sick of this bloody carry-on every night.'

Well, you shouldn't have a bloody karaoke machine if you don't want it used, you old grouch, Donna thought. She didn't say anything, though, just slouched back to the bar.

The American was waiting for her. Sweat slicked his Hawaiian shirt to his chest, and made dark patches under his armpits. He patted her hand. 'Look, how about some dinner?' Donna stared at him. He wasn't that bad, she thought. He had nice crinkly eyes, even if he was losing his hair. For a second she was tempted. 'Right now,' he pleaded.

She'd lose her job. And that was without thinking about Dave. 'No – Miseryguts won't give us the night off. Sorry.'

'Screw him,' the American said. 'Come on.' For a second she wavered. He was only taking advantage because she was upset. He was a bloke, and that was what blokes did, after all. But for a second it had seemed as if he really wanted to cheer her up. And it would be so nice to have a bit of company – just someone to talk to, mind, no funny business. Someone to talk to who wasn't knackered from a day on sentry duty or scrubbing out toilets or the other shit jobs Dave always seemed to get landed with. Someone who would pay a bit of attention to her.

But there had been other times she had been tempted the same way – like that time she'd snogged that fella at an off-limits nightclub back in England, and when she'd got home it turned out Dave was suffering from blood poisoning. She'd promised herself – and Dave – that she wasn't going to do anything like that again.

Besides, what was the point of singing about standing by your man if you weren't going to do it? 'No, better not,' she muttered, without looking at the American.

172

From behind her Pete called out in a sing-song voice, 'She's married!'

Bloody cheek of the bloody man, Donna thought, just as the American yelled, 'Butt out!' He turned back to her. 'How about it?'

'No thanks,' said Pete from behind her. He clinked a double handful of dirty glasses down on the bar.

Ha bloody ha, Donna thought. Putting words in her mouth like she was a kid who couldn't take care of herself. 'Yeah,' she said. 'Good idea.' The American's face lit up. 'Only dinner, mind,' she added quickly.

The American stood up. 'That's all I'm offering, honey.' He spread his hands out wide, like a cop on a TV show proving he was unarmed.

'If you go, don't expect to come back,' Pete said, as if he were pronouncing a death sentence.

Donna stripped off the Union Jack overall. She shoved it at him. 'Yeah? Well, what about me pay?' She glared at him, arms akimbo. She was suddenly aware of the skimpiness of her halterneck tee-shirt and the way the American was staring at her. And she realized she didn't mind at all.

'You!' shouted the American. When Pete looked up, he continued, 'Give the lady what she's due.'

Pete glared at both of them. His eyes drifted slightly south of Donna's face. 'I'd like to, believe me.'

Donna wasn't quite sure if that was meant as a compliment or not. She smiled uncertainly at the American. He smirked at her, and there was no doubt in his expression at all.

* * *

In the locker-room, the medic worked over the older illegal's injuries. The wound on his leg was deep and long. It was puffy with pus, and the edges of it had curled back to reveal the muscle beneath. It made Dave sick to look at it, and Paddy wasn't doing so well either. The illegal gripped the edge of the bench, and every so often as the medic wiped at the wound he clenched his hands so hard that his knuckles went white and his lips trembled.

The kid, dressed in a regulation issue tee-shirt a dozen sizes too big, hung on to the older lad's back, like a baby monkey clinging to its mother. He seemed fascinated by the medic's instruments. Eventually, the man gave him a bit of foil that one of the swabs had been wrapped in. You'd think it was gold from the way he grabbed it. He held it up to the light and turned it this way and that to make it glitter, then leaned forward and put it in front of the older illegal's face. The lad patted his hand in a clear gesture of re-assurance.

Dave fiddled with his sling, trying to get comfortable. It would be good for a couple of days off sick, he hoped. Always supposing he wasn't booted out.

'Amount of muck he's been through he'll need half a dozen jabs,' Paddy said.

Before Dave could say anything, Pereira's voice shouted, 'Tucker!' out of the darkness of the locker-room. He pounded up to them and crashed against the wire mesh partition, making it jangle. The kid was clearly terrified. He clung hard to the older lad's back and buried his face in his arms, whimpering.

174

'You've had it this time,' Pereira said to Dave. He sounded more resigned than angry. 'The Colonel's office. Now.'

He ran back the way he came without waiting for an answer, passing Tony, who was just arriving.

The Sergeant spread his arms wide. 'The interpreter's going to tell them about the gun anyway,' he said. He jerked his thumb at the illegal. 'And we can't speak Cantonese so we can't tell him not to, can we?'

Dave didn't say anything. It was only what he'd expected, after all.

'Yeah, mate,' Paddy said. He sounded disgusted. You want to watch that, Dave thought. You'll never get that third stripe if you go round seeing the squaddies' point of view all the time.

'What?' Tony said in an injured tone. 'I had a right bollocking, I did.' Dave started out of the locker room. As he went, Tony glared at him. 'This is going to hold up my substantive rank, this is.' Dave ignored him. There was nothing to say, really, and the Colonel was waiting.

As he got to the locker-room door, he heard Paddy say, 'My heart bleeds – '

He went out into the night and left them to argue about it.

So that's that then, Dave thought as he walked across the compound. He felt his stomach knot and a sour taste fill his mouth. Well, it wouldn't be so bad. They'd ship him back to England. That would please Donna. And if they kicked him out there was always security work. At least he had some experience now, not like when he'd joined up. Still, there'd be an unpleasant few weeks to get through before it came to that.

He went into the administration block. Lieutenant Pereira was already there, just about to go through the open door to Colonel Fortune's office. He grimaced at Dave just as Colonel Fortune called out, 'What can I do for you, Alex?'

The Lieutenant went in, closing the door behind him. Dave fiddled desperately with his sling, trying to get at least a bit comfortable and wondering if it might buy him a bit of a sympathy vote.

Just as he finished, the padre came in. 'Not outside the headmaster's office again.' He shook his head in mock – or perhaps real – despair, and went through to his own office.

Any minute now, Dave thought. Right on cue the Colonel roared, 'Right, that's it. Get them up here now.' It was impressive even through the closed door.

The American's name was Norman. Norm for short. He took Donna to the poshest Chinese restaurant she'd ever been to – all red-and-gold paper lanterns, and flock paper on the walls. It was full of Chinese people, too. That was a good sign, Norm said – it meant the food was authentic. Donna didn't know so much about that, but she thought the little gilt shell bowls that held the soap in the loo was dead canny, and they had nice thick towels to dry your hands on, too – none of those poxy warm-air driers that never quite got your hands dry.

176

As for Norm, he wasn't so bad. She left the ladies and threaded her way back to their table. This had been a brilliant idea, she decided. Just the thing to cheer her up. So long as Norm knew how to take a hint when the evening was over.

Norm was drinking schnapps from a tiny glass. 'Here she is,' he said as Donna sat down. He poured her a drink.

'You'll have me pissed,' she said. 'First lager, now this.' He smiled as if that was the furthest thing from his mind. They clinked glasses and she downed her drink in one. It burned her throat and left a lovely warm feeling in its wake. 'What we having?' Donna asked, to change the subject.

'There's only one thing to have in this place. It's famous for it. It's called garoupa.' Donna stared blankly at him. It sounded like a nickname for a dance partner with fifteen hands. 'It's a fish,' he explained.

Donna wasn't too keen on fish, but what the hell – you had to pitch in and make an effort if you wanted to have a good time, she reckoned. 'Ooh lovely,' she said. 'I'm just in the mood for a fish supper.' She thought about it a bit. 'Is it like cod? I mean, haddock's okay and that, but you sometimes get that skin stuff, don't you? And if there's one thing I'm a bit funny about – ' A waiter shoved a plate under her nose. There was a slimy great fish on it. It fluttered a fin at Donna, and opened and shut its pink little mouth. She screamed and leapt back, sending the chair flying.

Norm smiled indulgently at her. Bastard, she thought.

The Colonel was well pissed off. He hadn't called Dave in at all to begin with. Instead he'd made him wait outside and sent for Tony as well. So now they were both facing him and Pereira, and it was Dave's opinion that only the presence of the padre – who was currently standing at the back of the room, behind Dave and Tony – was likely to stop it from turning into a lynching party.

The Old Man had already told them in detail what he thought of them, but apparently he hadn't quite got it out of his system. He glared at Dave. 'This is another court-martial offence. Are you going for the record?' he bellowed. It was all Dave could do not to flinch visibly. The Colonel leaned across the desk and craned his neck so he could see the clerk at the ops desk in the office beyond. Dave could just imagine how hard the man was concentrating on his work. 'You out there! Take a break.' Too late, Dave thought. It would be all over the camp ten minutes after he got to the mess. The Old Man came round the side of the desk. 'Sergeant Wilton will be on a charge for not reporting the incident – '

'Sir, I – ' Tony tried and failed to interrupt.

It was his fault, Dave thought. The whole damn thing was down to Dave the fuck-up Tucker. Again. And any minute now he'd have to explain, but he didn't have an explanation. A pulse started to beat at his temple.

' - and Corporal Garvey for collusion. The whole damn platoon will have to search the area – '

For a split second Dave thought the Old Man had spoken to him, had told him to tell his side of it. 'Well, I was in a bit of a state, sir,' Dave said. The words came from out of nowhere. 'She's doing away with me kid – ' His voice slid up an octave. He was horrified to find that he was almost crying, horrified that he was speaking without permission.

'Oh, for crying out loud – ' the Old Man said.

Now the words had started, Dave just couldn't stop them. 'She's only twenty miles away but she might as well be in Newcastle for all I can do about it.' He stared desperately at the Colonel. 'Look, I'm sorry. But everything seemed all wrong and then he set the dog on them – '

'The dog just went for the gun hand, sir, like it's been trained – ' Tony cut in loudly.

'Yes, but the lad didn't know the dog was trained,' Tucker shouted over the top of him.

'No one would have got hurt if – ' Tony yelled.

'Shut up,' bellowed the Colonel.

'Sir,' said the padre from the back of the room.

'Not now, padre,' the Old Man said impatiently. He stared at the man for a moment. For a second, Dave thought his expression softened. But that was just hoping for too much. He found that he was shaking. He badly needed to pee, and his hands kept clenching and unclenching and he couldn't stop them.

The Colonel started back round the desk. Lieutenant Pereira was standing at attention near the wall.

'Mr Pereira,' Colonel Fortune said. 'Get this man back to Stanley. My office, Monday morning.' He leaned across the desk and glared at Dave. 'Between now and then sort your sodding marital affairs out.' He glanced from Dave to Tony. 'Now get out of my office, both of you.'

'Sir,' Tony said. He came to attention. So did Dave. They did an about-face and marched out, followed by Pereira.

Outside, Dave wanted to apologize. He stared at Tony, but he just couldn't find the words.

Garoupa – that would be a good name for Norm, Donna decided. He was all over her, trying not just for a kiss but to grope her bust. She shoved him away, hard, and he staggered back, then immediately tried to come back for the re-match. Donna pulled away and got a few yards between them. He came on again.

'I'll scratch your eyes out,' she said. 'All I said was dinner.'

She'd known that coming to Kowloon Park was a mistake. It was very pretty – full of little streams that flowed between flower beds and paved paths, and lanterns on poles, and fountains that caught the light like a million fragments of diamond. But it was also full of couples courting decorously and not so decorously under paper parasols and on the stone benches that were dotted through the park.

'Look. Look,' Norm said from behind her. 'What are they all doing?'

'They're all watching us, you prat,' she whispered. 'You're showing us up.'

'It's a little kiss,' Norm insisted. 'They're all doing it.'

Well, maybe they were, Donna thought. But they weren't Donna Tucker. 'They're not all drunk and they're not all over each other.' She knew she should just tell him to piss off, but her heart just wasn't in it.

'Okay,' he said, coming up behind her. 'I'm enthusiastic. I'm an extrovert – ' At least he didn't try to touch her again.

Here we go. Mr Poser makes his great comeback, Donna thought. He'd seemed better during dinner. At least once she'd persuaded him to take her to a place where the food didn't talk back at you. She might have known it wouldn't last.

'And married,' she said without looking at him. Suddenly she remembered Dave – not as he' d been when they'd fought at the barbecue, but before, when they'd walked hand in hand by the waterfront. That way he had of laughing. The scrappy little bit of hair on his chest. The length of his fingers – not a soldier's hands, she'd always said. A pianist's, maybe. She thought about all that, and she thought about Norm panting after her, and she felt sick to her stomach. 'I'm going home now,' she said, hoping he'd finally get the hint. She started to walk tiredly down the path.

'Okay,' he said, still behind her. 'I'm married. If I wasn't – Jesus, you think I'd be doing this?'

Charmed, I'm sure, Donna thought. But it was true. If she hadn't been married and pissed off with her husband, she'd never have gone off with a man like Norm. 'I'm married too,' she murmured.

Norm came up to stand beside her, but he didn't try to touch her. 'Yeah, miseryguts said so.'

'He's a soldier on the border,' Donna said. When you put it like that, it almost sounded romantic. It certainly sounded terrible that she'd almost been unfaithful. If Norm had taken things a bit slower . . . she thought. But he hadn't, so there was nothing to worry about. Nothing to have to admit to Dave.

'Jeez, that's tough,' Norm said. They strolled down the path together. 'At least Marie's home with her folks.' He paused. 'Safe in Ohio.' For the first time since Donna had known him, Norm seemed sincere.

She grinned at him. 'Not New York?'

He grinned back – a nice smile. Donna thought, if he'd been like this all along, things might have been different. She was really glad he hadn't been. He gestured at a bench next to a fountain. 'Look – you want to sit down?'

They went to the bench and sat on it, careful not to touch. Norm crossed his arms. Donna stared at the lights strung out through the park.

Norm sighed. 'I've been all over, and it makes me crazy. Airports. Hotels. Strangers. Nobody to talk to – to say "Wow – look at that!"' He flung his hands out. 'You got to be cool, you know –' Donna didn't, not really. She wondered what he did that made him travel, if he hated it so much. 'You got to act like you've seen it all,' he went on. He laughed. 'I'm from a dinky little town in Ohio . . .'

Somewhere in the middle, Donna thought. She had a vague picture in her head of rolling grassland and vast fields of corn. He hadn't been lying about the prairie, then. What did she miss? Her mam's little terraced house and Newcastle covered market of a Saturday morning. Bacon butties and nice cool cloudy days, though she'd never have guessed it back home. 'I'm from Newcastle, me.' Norm didn't say anything. Donna tried to think of a way of describing it, but she couldn't. 'It's a canny place.' That said it all, really. She smiled at the thought. She never did work out what put it into her head to ask, but she said, 'Have you got any kids?'

'Marie wants them,' Norm said. 'But I'd be . . .' he stumbled as if he were embarrassed. 'I'd be a lousy dad.'

'I bet you wouldn't,' Donna said, smiling. Earlier, she would have agreed with him; but this Norm who missed his wife was very different. She could see him throwing a frisbee around in some American park. Or kicking a football . . . Dave would like that, she thought. She'd never thought of what kind of father Dave would make. Only that it would hurt a lot and screw up their lives. 'My Dave wouldn't,' she said. She thought about how he'd be . . . if it was a girl, he'd spoil her rotten, want her dressed up in pretty clothes all the time. And if it were a boy, he'd still spoil him, but he'd want to wrestle with him, and show him how to get right mucky messing around with cars . . . and of course, whatever it was you'd never be able to get Dave to do the telling off. 'He'd be dead soft,' she said wistfully.

He wanted it so much – to be a dad, because he'd never had a family of his own.

Norm broke into her thoughts. 'Come on – I'll walk you home.'

They wandered down towards the ferry. 'She good-looking, your Marie?' Donna asked, just to be making conversation.

'She's okay,' Norm said.

For a second, Donna was taken aback – it didn't seem a very nice way to talk about your wife. But then she saw the look on his face, and it was obvious that he thought the world of her.

'Dave's a bit like a young Sting,' she said. She considered. 'Without the ponytail.'

It was a bit of an exaggeration. But only a little one.

Dave sat in the back of the truck that was going to take him back to Stanley. His kitbag was at his feet. If there was a way out of this mess, he couldn't see it. And as for Donna – well, it wouldn't surprise him if he got home and found she'd already got rid of the bairn.

Something nudged his calf. He looked down. Midnight was staring up at him. Oh, piss off if you've come to have another go, Dave thought. But he was too weary to say it.

'Wotcha, Dave,' Midnight said. 'All right?' When Dave didn't answer, he went on, 'That was a good try with the kids, mate.' Yeah, yeah, Dave thought. He wondered if Paddy had had a word with him, and then decided he didn't care. A friend was a friend, after all. Someone started yelling in the jungle outside the base, and there were crashing and tearing sounds. 'That's another lot coming over by the sounds of it,' Midnight said. 'You're well out of it.' He walked off in the direction of the barracks.

Out of it, Dave thought. Yeah, that's what I am. Probably permanently.

His driver slammed the tailgate of the lorry shut, blocking out his view of the camp.

Nancy thought it was all a great adventure. She and Joy had been waiting up for Donna when she got back. For an awful second she thought Mela had told them how she'd tried to get an abortion, but if she had they didn't let on. All Joy said was that they'd been worried about her after the barbecue, and that sounded about right. If Joy didn't have something to worry about, she started worrying about it.

And so she'd told them all about Norm, and how he'd turned out to be nice after all. Joy had nipped out to check on Matthew, and, she said, to get a treat she'd been saving up.

'Then he'll be back in Ohio in a few days?' Nancy said. She was sitting on Donna's sofa with her hands behind her back.

Donna stared up at her from where she was sitting on the floor. 'He said the corn is as high as an elephant's eye,' she said.

Nancy grinned. 'I've heard that one too, somewhere,' she said quickly.

Donna thought about sitting next to Norm on the bench by the fountain, and of what she'd decided then. It had all seemed so simple . . . She sighed. 'God, I suppose I'm going to have this kid.'

Nancy grinned. Just at that moment, Joy came in the front door. She was holding baby Matthew on her hip with one hand, and in the other she had a plate. 'He was awake,' she explained.

She looked so right with him, Donna thought. She just couldn't see herself like that.

Before she could worry about it too much, Nancy leapt up. She went round to Joy and peered at the plate. 'Yeah!' she said. 'Ice cream cake – next best thing to sex, you know.' Donna looked at her but couldn't raise a smile. Nancy put her fist on her hip. 'The state you'll be in soon, you'll need the recipe.' She laughed coarsely. Oh, thanks very much, Donna thought. That really cheers us up, that does. She could feel Nancy staring at her, but she wouldn't look round. After a bit Nancy said, 'I'll just go and get some plates.'

She went across to Donna's kitchen, and Joy came and sat on the sofa. She was in her old purple dressing-gown, and her hair was a frazzled mess tied up with a bit of ribbon. Donna heaved herself up to sit next to her.

Matthew was plump and golden, with little pink cheeks and huge blue eyes. Donna stared at him like he was a new kind of animal she'd never seen before. 'What if I'm on my own – when I have it, like?' she said.

'Dave'll be there,' Joy said confidently.

Donna laughed shortly. 'Oh aye, I can really bet on that, can't I?'

'Course he will be,' Joy said. 'And if he isn't, one of us'll be, yeah?'

Nancy bustled in with plates of ice-cream cake. 'Yeah,' she said, handing them out. She plonked herself down next to Donna. 'There you go. You're never alone in the army.'

Donna stared at Matthew. He regarded her solemnly, clutching his teddy bear. His fingernails were like little specks of diamond dust. Joy nuzzled at his hair. He smelt of soap and talc and that odd baby smell, and his nose needed wiping but it didn't stop him looking adorable. If you were inclined that way.

'Oh I'm only going to be a sodding mam, aren't I?' Donna said. But somehow she wasn't nearly as unhappy about it as she thought she ought to be.

The lift stopped and Dave got out. He went over to his front door and pulled out his key. He put it in the lock but before he could turn it peals of hysterical laughter came from inside the flat.

Not again, he thought. If she had some man there, he didn't know what he'd do about it. He didn't feel up to a fight – not with her and certainly not with some yob she'd picked up in a bar. He laid his forehead against the cool wood, wondering what the hell to do next.

He walked away. He heard the door open behind him and swung round. Joy came out carrying Matthew, followed by Donna and Nancy. For a second they were so busy chatting and laughing that they didn't see him.

Then Donna spotted him. 'Dave! What happened to your arm?'

'An alsatian got us,' he muttered; but he thought, she does care. She does. She had to. What else was there left for him if she didn't?

For a couple of seconds, no one spoke, then Joy said her goodbyes, and Nancy did, and they were left alone staring at each other.

'Well, come in then,' Donna said. She opened the door a bit wider. Dave went inside. There was nothing else for him to do.

The weekend was tough, and the interview with Colonel Fortune even tougher, but somehow Dave managed to get through both of them.

Afterwards, he met Donna down by the waterfront. The early morning sun struck gold from the sea as they walked along the beach, like kids in their bare feet with the wet sand squelching up between their toes.

'You want to taste this cake stuff Joy brought round,' Donna said. 'I'm gonna make some. Think it's a craving, like.'

She sounded almost embarrassed about it. That would be the thought of her cooking, Dave decided. Well, they said pregnancy made women do strange things. 'Is it?' he said, just for something to say.

'Eee, I'll tell you what though – I've gone right off fish – '

'Have you?' Dave asked. He stared at her. She'd never seemed more beautiful to him. She'd been so scared, and what had he done? Yelled at her in front of all their friends. Screwed everything up all over again. 'Are you going to be all right?'

She looked at him, and for a second that scared look was back in her eyes. It made him think of the little Chinese kid. 'I don't know,' she said.

He didn't say anything for a minute. They just walked in silence, and he thought – she's that scared, but she's going ahead with it for me. What the hell did he have that he could put beside that? 'I love you,' he said at last.

He could feel her staring at him. 'I missed you,' she said.

She always did. He couldn't do anything about it. There would always be times when the army sent him away. It was like a knife turning in his heart.

She reached out and touched the bandage round his hand, very gently. 'You going to be in trouble again?'

He'd been waiting for this. 'Well,' he started gravely, 'the Old Man's fined us so much money he'll be able to buy a tank.' She stared at him, waiting for the rest of it. But there was no rest of it – he didn't understand why, or what had made him change his mind, but there it was. He grinned.

Donna finally caught on. She leaned towards him. 'Perhaps they'll put our names on it,' she said. She spread her hand to indicate what she meant – a windscreen. '"Donna and Dave".'

Dave backed away slowly. 'And one of them signs on the back,' he said when he was far enough away. '"Baby on board".'

He waited for the explosion. It didn't come. She just stood looking at her fingers. It was going to be a long while before she was really happy with the idea. What had the padre said? *Give her time.* Well at least now there was enough time to do it.

She turned slowly and came towards him. He backed off a bit further, so he was standing in the water.

'You'd fall in a cesspit and come up smelling of roses, you would,' she said, still advancing on him.

'Funny you should say that,' Dave said. He kicked a bit of water at her, and she kicked some at him, and then they were running through the water and splashing each other like kids.

Paddy had said that if he wanted to be a dad, he should grow up first. Well, he would.

Tomorrow.

Chapter 10

Moonlight glinted on the water below the terrace of Stanley boathouse, which had been decked out with fairy lights and streamers while music blared out from a sound system in the corner. The next day there was going to be a charity tournament – silly races, mostly – to raise funds for the local children's homes, and the Old Man wanted everyone in a good mood for it, especially with all the locals and journalists that were going to be there.

Dave grabbed a couple of cans – one for him and one for Donna, who was waiting over by the barbecue with Nancy and Paddy. Next to him, Tony and Joy Wilton and Midnight Rawlings did the same. Dave tore the ringpull of his can open, and started to follow the others back.

Funny how fast Hong Kong had started to seem like home, Dave thought. When they'd first arrived he'd thought he'd never get used to the terrible heat and humidity, and the smell of rotting vegetables that seemed to get into everything. Now that seemed normal – and this felt just like a party on a nice summer's night would back at home. Then he realized just how long they'd been there: it was hard to believe it was eighteen months. Well, to be precise nineteen months, three weeks and two days. It felt like no time at all, and half a lifetime. A couple of weeks ago, he'd thought he might not make the full two years, but that was behind him now.

Easy streets from now on, he thought. A nice few months with no worries would round out the tour nicely. Take this Helping Hands Day fête the army was putting on to raise money for charity. It wasn't so much work as fun – especially since Number 1 Platoon had been drawn to go up against the wives' team. Piece of piss, the lads reckoned, and if Dave hadn't seen the glint in Donna's eye when she talked about it, he'd have been inclined to agree.

Not that it was all roses, mind you; but at least this time it wasn't Dave that was deep in the brown stuff. This time it was Major Cochrane, of all people – he'd been dating a much younger girl from a wealthy Chinese family, and she'd accused him of assaulting her.

Tony was taking it particularly hard – the Major had come up through the ranks, and Dave supposed the Sergeant had seen himself following in the officer's footprints. As they started to thread their way across the crowded terrace to where Donna and the Garveys were waiting, he raised the subject. Again.

'It's his wife I feel sorry for,' Joy said.

'He hasn't got a wife,' Tony pointed out. 'She left him. They're divorced.'

Aye well, Dave thought. Maybe Joy had a point anyway – you had to wonder why she'd left in the first place.

'Well, what about the Chinese girl, poor thing?' Midnight said.

Typical Midnight, Dave reckoned. One of life's great romantics, he was. It would get him in trouble one of these days. And of course, he did have a point –

'Leave it out, Midnight,' Tony said. 'Can you imagine Major Cochrane beating up a girl? He's been stitched up.' He said it like the jury had already brought in their verdict.

Dave was too far away to make himself heard, or he would have said something about it. But Tony did have a point. Cochrane was not a particularly nice piece of work – he was a sarcastic bastard when the mood took him, and he bore a grudge like no officer Dave had come across – but he was army through and through. He was proud of having made officer, let alone Major, and he was always lecturing the men on how an officer ought to behave.

Before he could say anything, Joy cut in. 'They don't like us, you know. They reckon we sold them down the river.' She looked up at Tony. 'I reckon this time it's the other way round.'

Dave went over to Donna. She was standing by the barbecue, next to Paddy. He was dancing around, turning the sausages over in time to the music. He tossed Donna her can, then parked himself up against the railings just in time to see Joy leading Tony out on to the dance floor with a determined look on her face.

Paddy looked at them. 'Looks like Joy's only got one thing on her mind – again,' he said, deftly flipping a piece of steak over.

'Aye well, if my husband gambled all our money away, I'd have a thing to say about it, too,' Donna said.

'Me too,' Nancy chipped in from behind Paddy. 'Specially if I'd already gone and spent it –'

'From what I heard, she had a bit of help in that department,' Dave said. Joy had bought a leather sofa, which she could only afford because Nancy had haggled with the shop owner. Unfortunately, Tony had tried to ante five hundred pounds into twelve hundred by gambling on a wrestling match. He'd lost the lot – which was a shame, because the original five hundred was enough to cover the cost of the sofa.

'Oh give over,' Donna said. 'Let's talk about something else – like how the wives' team's going to grind you lot into the dust.'

Paddy grinned at her but didn't answer. Instead he turned to Nancy. 'Honestly, Nance, when I heard we were up against the wives' team I was dead chuffed. We can put our feet up now.'

'Easy,' Dave chanted, football-hooligan style.

'Oh, thank you very much,' Nancy said.

'Take no notice, Nance,' Donna said. She took a long swallow of her lager. 'They don't know what they're sodding talking about.'

Dave just grinned. If it made her happy, he was happy too.

'There's a lot of money riding on us getting through to the second round,' Paddy said. He glanced over to the dance floor, where Tony and Joy were doing more talking than smooching, then gave the onion pan a quick shake.

'Gonna get tough out there,' Dave said. He raised his can in a mock toast.

'I'm only warning you,' Paddy said.

'Promises promises,' Nancy put in.

Donna turned to Dave. 'That's what we live on, mate.'

Dave grinned at her. Now that things had settled down between them, he would have promised her the sun, the moon and the stars to keep her happy. Even if he did have to make the stars out of tinfoil.

So the men thought they were going to have an easy time of it, did they? Donna grinned to herself. Not if she had anything to do with it. She with Rachel Fortune and Joy and the other wives just behind them.

The first race in the Helping Hands Challenge was ready to go – a slalom jeep race ending up with a straight run for the finishing tape. Nancy was going to drive for the wives, against Paddy for Number 1 Platoon. They stood across the way, next to the jeeps which had been decorated with balloons and streamers.

The Old Man stood between them. He was umpiring. If you could trust a man not to cheat. 'All set?' he called out.

'All set,' Paddy and Nancy chorused. They moved up to the marks.

'On your marks . . . get set – ' The Colonel blew his whistle.

Before Paddy could move, Nancy reached out and

gave his balls a good pinch. He yelped and she was off, racing for her jeep. Paddy hobbled to his.

'Up the girls,' Donna yelled. 'Nancy! Nan-cy!' She waved a bit of streamer above her head. She poked Joy in the ribs. 'She's canny lass, eh Joy?'

'What? Oh. Yes.'

Nancy started down the course, handling the heavy jeep easily enough. Paddy got into his – and immediately reversed. Poor lad, Donna thought. The shock of it's got him all confused. Joy didn't even laugh.

'What's the matter, pet?' Donna asked. 'You look like you lost a tenner and found fifty pence –'

Joy wrinkled her nose up. 'Lost a leather sofa and found a set of golf clubs, more like.' She sighed. 'We won them in the raffle. I was just wondering how much we'd get for them – if we can sell them at all.'

'Not enough to pay for your sofa, if that's what you mean,' Donna said, and immediately regretted it. Oh well, she thought. It's too late now.

She looked back at the race. Nancy was just rounding the last slalom post, while on his side Paddy had two to go.

'Come on,' Rachel yelled. The jeep swept past them, and they had to run to get to it.

The men's jeep rolled up, but it couldn't get to the end of the course.

'Bloody hell, Nance!' Donna shouted as she clambered aboard.

'Don't knock it,' Rachel said. She reached over to pat Nancy on the shoulder just as she gunned the engine. Donna's expression must have let on that she didn't understand, because Rachel turned back and said, 'Stopped the men from getting to the end – look!'

Donna did. Sure enough, the men had had to wait for Nancy to move before they could get into position to load up.

Nancy looked over her shoulder and winked. 'That'll teach Paddy Garvey to try and let me win,' she said.

'Oh aye,' Donna said. She turned to Joy and said, 'Win any way you can, that's what I say, hey pet?'

Joy's face lit up. 'Do you think we can?' she asked. 'I mean, it's only two more races, isn't it?'

'Don't see why not,' Donna said, 'They're only men, after all.' It was then that she remembered the conversation she'd overheard between Dave and Paddy. What had Paddy said just before Dave spotted her and told him to shut up? *That prat's only talking about putting money on the wives to win . . .*

Well we'll have to see about that, won't we pet? she thought at Joy.

The first race had been a bloody embarrassment, so it was just as well they'd made it up with a clear win in the second one, Dave thought. Mind you, if Paddy had screwed up in the first one, it had been Tony's show in the second. Build a bridge between weighted oil-drums in a roped off part of the bay, using only two planks and a length of rope, then carry one member of the team across it.

Easy-peasy.

It had been the girls' brains against the lads' brawn. For a while it had looked as if Paddy's approach – throwing the planks at the drums and hoping they hit – would keep them clear ahead, specially since the girls insisted on behaving like they were Sappers building a bridge fit to take an entire armoured division. Slow and sure, that's what Rachel yelled to them – but it looked like coming unstuck until Tony started blundering around and knocked the planks skewiff. Then Joy – of all people, considering everything – managed to lose her balance as she was helping to carry Donna across. She didn't just fall in the water, she brought the whole of the wives' bridge down, and they hadn't even managed to get hold of the planks before the lads had raced ashore.

If it hadn't been for that, he might have started to believe Paddy when he said that Tony had put money on the wives to win – specially when he saw the look of fury on the Sergeant's face as the Old Man announced that they'd won. Either Paddy was wrong or there was going to be one hell of a battle in the Wiltons' flat later on, he mused.

He took a swig of lager. Not long now and it would be all over. They were just waiting for the other heats to finish, so they could start the last race. Just time to wind Donna up. He looked around. Tony and Joy were deep in conversation, but Nancy was standing by herself.

He ambled over to her. 'Have you seen my Donna, Nancy?' he asked.

'Not for a bit,' she said. 'She said she felt a bit headachey, so she was going to sit in the shade — '

'But she's all right, isn't she?' Dave asked. It was never far from his thoughts that she was pregnant, even though she wasn't showing it yet.

'Oh yes,' Nancy said. 'Don't worry about her.' She giggled. 'You've got enough on your plate with the canoe race . . .'

'Oh aye,' Dave said. He was going to say something sarky, but before he could think of anything she spotted Paddy coming towards her and went over to him.

Dave turned. A glint of sunlight on glass drew his attention upwards. Major Cochrane was standing at an upper window of the officers' quarters. It was difficult to be really sure at this distance, but Dave thought he looked as miserable as sin.

So it was true then, he thought — the Major was being kicked out.

'Come on, Dave,' Paddy said. 'We're on!'

Donna settled into her place at the back of the wives' canoe. She picked up her drumsticks and gave an experimental little taradiddle on the tambour she was supposed to use to beat time. The shore was quite a way off, but she was certain they'd be okay. They'd practised for long enough, after all.

'You ready then, girls?' Paddy shouted from the men's canoe. He was sitting at the front, with Dave.

'Oh aye,' she shouted back. 'You just watch us — '

All they had to do was win this one race and the

men would be buying them drinks for the next month, she reckoned. It would be worth all their effort just to see the expression on their faces.

'Ready!' the Old Man shouted. The whistle blew before Donna was quite ready for it, and she didn't get the rhythm with the drumsticks just right.

Not to worry, the girls were keeping time very nicely, thank you very much, Paddy Garvey. Besides, the men were bellowing the theme tune to *Hawaii 5–0*, complete with frequent pauses to yell, 'Book 'im, Dano.'

She grinned. They probably thought the women had no chance of beating them, even if they did piss around. They were a good length and a bit ahead, after all. Well, that was going to change any minute . . .

Now!

Sure enough, Dave held up his paddle. The blade had broken off. So had Paddy's. And Tony's. 'What the bloody hell!' one of them yelled, and then they were all shouting and trying to paddle with their hands.

'Thank God!' Nancy yelled, looking skyward.

'Don't thank Him,' Donna said. She reached into her bag and held up the hacksaw she'd used on the men's paddles. 'Brains and initiative, kidder,' she said.

The women howled with glee and paddled like crazy. They quickly overtook the men – so quickly that they were still laughing when they got ashore and the Old Man announced that he was declaring the race null and all bets void.

Joy looked glum. 'I thought we might have been out of trouble,' she said to Donna as they walked over to join the men. 'You might have done something a little bit more subtle, Donna!'

'Well, thank you very much,' Donna said, but she was smiling.

Dave came over. He grinned at her. 'I'll remember this the next time you say you've got a headache,' he said.

Donna smiled sweetly. 'That doesn't happen as often as your paddle getting broken, now does it pet?' she asked.

For an answer he grabbed her and swung her in close. 'I'll talk to you about that later, all right?'

Afterwards, they all walked home together. Tony really had won a set of golf clubs in the raffle, like Donna said he had. Major Cochrane had donated them, Tony said – they were a top-quality set. That turned the conversation sour for a bit, as they remembered he hadn't been at the Challenge because he was on a charge. But the day had been too good for any rotten mood to last long, and eventually they all cheered up again.

Tony admitted he'd put money on the wives' team to win, and Dave just grinned when Joy said it was the kind of thing he'd get up to. He put his arm around his bright, beautiful Donna's waist and was thoroughly grateful she was still with him. They dropped back a bit to watch the boats in the bay, when there was a sudden howl from Joy.

Three Chinese men were bringing a grey leather sofa out of the married quarters towards an open removal van. Two of them were more like mountains than men, but the third one was a wrinkled little raisin of a man in a sharp suit.

'That'll be Joy's little shopping spree then,' he said. They came up beside Paddy and Nancy to watch what happened, while Tony and Joy argued with the men. Except they weren't arguing, but clinging bodily to the sofa while the men tried to move it.

'It'll end in tears,' Dave said.

'You no want to pay,' said the elderly Chinese gentleman.

'Well do something then, you two great lummoxes,' Nancy said.

'Give over, Nance,' Paddy said. 'If they can't pay for it they can't pay and it'll just have to go back.'

'I haven't got any money,' Tony yelled at the top of his voice. The men inched closer to the removal van. Joy clung on as if it would save her life, but it only slowed them a little.

'Just what friends are for, eh Nance,' Donna said. She fanned herself languidly with her hand.

'Look,' Tony yelled. 'Let's go upstairs and talk about it.' He jabbed his finger in the direction of his flat.

'All right,' said the old man. He slapped the seat of the sofa and the mountain-men put it down.

Tony started to swing the clubs off his shoulder. The old man grabbed at them. 'You give me this,' he said.

'Oy!' Tony said. 'Leave that!'

'Funny,' Paddy said. 'He wasn't that attached to them a minute ago.'

'Aye,' said Donna, 'but that was before Mr Triad was trying to nick them – '

'Oh Donna,' Nance said, 'they aren't the Triads.'

'Wanna bet?'

Nobody did.

Meanwhile, Tony was having a hard time keeping the old man away from his clubs. 'Get your hands off,' he said, turning to keep his body between the clubs and the mountain-men. 'These are very expensive.' Dave almost saw the light dawn visibly in his eyes. 'Nick Faldo's played with these. They were a birthday present to him from Sevi Balesteros – '

The old man said something too soft and rapid for Dave to catch.

'Part payment?' Tony said. 'All right.' He slapped the back of the sofa. 'Take this back upstairs and we'll talk about it.'

The mountain-men picked the sofa up and started to haul it back inside. Joy leapt up and down, hanging on to Tony and squeaking like an excited puppy.

Dave turned to Donna. 'What's that you're always saying about me and cesspits, pet?'

Donna grinned. 'You and the company you keep, hin.'

Paddy went over to Tony, and the others followed him. 'See you for a drink later, mate?'

'Once you've got this sorted out, like,' Dave added, jerking his thumb at the removal van.

'Nah,' Tony said. 'I can't. Not tonight. I have to go and see the Major off.'

There was an awkward silence, and after a bit they all went in without saying much.

That's the trouble with cesspits, Dave thought as they waited for the lift. Every so often someone falls in one and comes up smelling of shit.

Chapter 11

A thunderflash exploded somewhere to Dave's left. He signalled to Midnight to come and cover him. As soon as the other man arrived, he broke and ran up the ridge towards the tank they were supposed to be taking out.

Gunfire rattled on his right. He dropped to cover and rattled off a few rounds from his own SA80, then snaked forward on his belly. They were up there somewhere . . . today's designated enemy. The yellow blank-firing attachment on his rifle barrel didn't make life any easier – it stood out like a beacon against the sandy scrub. Still, it was the same for the other bastards.

The tank was only ten metres away, and it looked good and dead. But you never could tell . . .

Do it by the book, he thought. You know they want to see if you can.

He signalled again to Midnight, who stood up and more or less strolled over to him. Dave grabbed his leg and yanked him down. 'You want to get this stripe or not, Midnight?' he hissed.

'All the same to me, mate,' Midnight said. His face glistened with sweat, and his camo was almost invisible against the darkness of his skin.

'Well, just get over there and take that tank out, will you?' Dave whispered. 'Cos I do want it.'

'Yeah, yeah, yeah,' Midnight said. He got up and walked towards the tank.

'Try crawling, Midnight,' Dave said, properly narked.

Midnight turned, letting his weapon swing free. He chomped on his wad of gum. 'Tank's dead,' he said.

Like hell. 'I wouldn't bank on it,' Dave said.

'Look it's too bloody hot,' Midnight sneered.

Right on cue a Fusilier stuck his head out of the turret.

'Shit!' Dave screamed. He opened fire on the enemy just as the enemy fired on Midnight. Their SA80s rattled at each other for a few seconds. At least Midnight had the sense to drop to his knees out of the way. Dave broke off the exchange. He pulled out a thunderflash, primed it and hurled it in the general direction of the tank.

'. . . two, one,' Dave thought. The thunderflash let out a dull *whump* and smoke billowed out of it. Dave used the cover to run forward firing. The tank never stood a chance.

Jack stripe? Junior NCO cadre? No problem, he thought.

It took Dave all of half an hour after the end of the training exercise to stop being pissed off with Midnight. After all, if people had held it against him every time he screwed up, he wouldn't have had any mates at all. And having just had another row with Donna –

who'd ended up throwing him out altogether this time – he reckoned he needed all the mates he could get.

Besides, poor old Midnight wasn't having a good time of it, not with the news he'd just had from home.

But all of that couldn't ruin Dave's mood. Not when he'd seen the expression on old Paella's face when he took out that tank. So he clapped his hands as he approached the table on the terrace outside the mess where Tony and Paddy were lazing around and said, 'Right, who's for a piss-up, then?'

'Oh sod off,' Tony said, taking a sip of something that looked suspiciously like orange juice.

'Don't look at me,' Paddy said. 'Not after last night – '

'Well, don't all rush at once,' Dave said, seeing his celebration disappearing. A bit more encouragement was obviously needed. He slapped an arm round Midnight's shoulder. 'This lad here – ' he laid his head against the taller man's shoulder, ' – this lad here got a letter from back home today – from his fiancée.' Midnight lit up a cigarette. He didn't look straight at any of them. 'She's given him the chocolate watch.' Dave straightened up.

'Oh no, mate,' Paddy said. You could always rely on Paddy for a bit of sympathy.

But not Tony. 'Is that why you messed up the exercise, Midnight?' He took a sip of his drink and pulled an evil face.

'I was going to give her the elbow anyway,' he said, but he didn't sound very convinced about it.

'Course you were,' Tony said. He drained his glass.

'So in other words you're completely gutted,' Paddy said , squinting up at him.

Midnight took a drag of his cigarette instead of answering.

'So,' Dave said, 'we've got to take him out and get him rat-arsed.' The others stared at him. 'It's traditional, isn't it?'

'Well . . . it is sort of expected,' Paddy said, getting into the idea.

'No, not me,' Tony said, 'Joy'll go bananas.'

'Take your time, lads,' Dave said. He stared at Paddy. Hen pecked or what? he let his expression say.

Paddy finished his drink in one swallow and stood up. 'Sod it,' he said and banged his glass down on the table. 'Let's go.'

That's more like it, he thought. 'I've heard of this great place,' he said. 'Nightclub, massage parlour – ' he turned to lead the way, ' – and knocking shop all under one roof.'

'All back to your place then, is it?' Tony said, following him.

Dave grinned at him. 'Madame Chow's,' he said.

Knocking shop. That'd teach Donna a lesson.

'Don't worry,' Joy said. She put the mug of tea down in front of Donna. 'He'll come round, you'll see.'

'Oh aye,' Donna said. She felt terrible – head like a lead balloon and eyes like red-hot coals. 'I'm just not sure I want him to – '

'You do really,' Joy said, with that cheery confidence that got right up Donna's nose. 'What did you argue about, anyway?'

'Sex,' Donna said, enjoying the shocked look on Joy's face. 'He was all hot and bothered about when he woke up, but I just didn't feel like it – I feel that sick of a morning, you know.' Her dressing-gown had risen up. She tugged it back into place.

She realized Joy was staring at her and glared right back. So what if it was seven o' bloody clock in the evening? There wasn't a hell of a lot to get up for, was there?

'But Donna, you kept saying you were scared he didn't fancy you because you'd put on weight,' Joy said.

'Don't you bloody start,' Donna snapped. She hadn't even invited the woman over.

'Well, if you're going to be like that – ' Joy started, but before she could finish there was a knock at the door. She raised an eyebrow at Donna.

'You go and get it then,' Donna said. 'I'm in me nightie.'

Joy did, and Nancy walked in. She was still in her uniform.

'I'll just make you a nice cup of tea,' Joy said.

Donna stared at her cup. There was a bit of scum floating on the surface. 'Oh, I don't know about that,' she said.

Nancy swept her cap off and put it on the table. 'You'll never guess what they've got me doing, girls,' she said.

'Surprise us,' Donna said.

'Interviewing blokes who've got the clap,' she said. 'Trying to get them to tell us which brothels they've been to and who was with them.' She giggled. 'The corporal they partnered me with can't handle it at all, poor lad.'

Joy handed her a cup of tea. 'I don't blame him,' she said. 'It sounds really disgusting.'

'Well, you would think so,' Donna said. Not that she wouldn't kill Dave if he ever got up to anything like that.

'And tonight I have to go out and talk to the girls – find out which ones are clean and which aren't. Mind you, it looks as if this lot have all been to the one place,' she said.

'Oh yeah,' Donna said. 'Where's that, then?'

'Place called Madame Chow's,' Nancy said.

Madame Chow's was all it was knocked up to be – soft lights, good music and pretty girls – at least if you squinted. A few men in suits were bopping around on the dance floor. Even as Dave watched from the entrance, one of them stopped dancing and whispered something to his partner. She smiled and played with his tie, then led him away upstairs.

A hostess with legs up to here and a leather dress with a big zip down the front came over. Dave stared at her and wondered what she'd do if he pulled the zip down right here and now. Probably charge him for the view. She ignored them and went over to a fat old man in a tuxedo.

Dave went inside. He looked around and clapped his hands. 'Is this the place or what?' he said.

Paddy and the others were already at the bar when he got there. A middle-aged Chinese woman wearing make-up so thick she must have employed a plasterer to put it on said, 'What you gonna have, boys.'

For someone who hadn't wanted to come out, Tony was getting into the swing of things pretty fast. He was already dancing around as he said, 'Four pints of lager please doll.'

The woman leaned across the bar. She smiled slyly at him. 'Have a Madame Chow's special,' she said. 'Guaranteed to blow your bleedin' heads off.' She had a husky voice brought on by years of gin and cigarettes. She'd have been a looker when she was younger, Dave reckoned.

Tony looked at Dave, then swivelled his eyes to Midnight. Paddy took a drag on his cigarette. 'Oh aye,' he said. 'What's in it?'

'Rum, gin, tequila and a special ingredient only from Madame Chow's,' the woman said.

Oh yeah, Dave thought. Tap water, no doubt. Everyone knew that was how these joints made their money.

'All right, doll,' Tony said. 'Four of them.'

Madame Chow went away, and after a bit she came back with four tall glasses. It was just as well they sounded the business, because they certainly didn't look it – not with all those little umbrellas and bits of fruit and frosting round the outside. Dave tasted his drink. It was a bit like fruit punch – probably didn't have much alcohol in it at all. He took a bigger swig and loped off in search of some action.

He found it, too, with a couple of beautiful Filipino girls. Not a lot up top, but with legs like that, they didn't need it. He danced for a bit, then decided it was time for a refill. He spotted Paddy and Midnight. They were sitting near the bar, talking – to each other. Tony was dancing behind them, also alone. Can't have that, he thought. They looked well on the way, but a bit more booze never hurt anyone.

'It was her parents – threatened to kick her out, see,' Midnight said. Dave took his glass from his unresisting hand.

'Why's that then?' Paddy said. He grinned stupidly and put his arm round Midnight's shoulder. 'Cos you drink too much?'

'Yeah, all right,' Midnight said. 'Cos I'm black and she's white.'

Tony leaned over them. 'Never mind, cocker,' he said. 'Plenty more pebbles out there on the beach.'

Dave stared down at Midnight. A hurt expression flickered across his face. Then he leaned back and said up to Tony, 'Ah, I was going to jack her in, anyway.'

Say it one more time and you'll start sounding like you mean it, Dave thought.

Midnight clambered to his feet. He swayed a bit, then steadied up. 'Four more of these, right?' He took his glass back off Dave. 'I'll come and give you a hand, mate.'

They went up to the bar. Dave ordered, but by the time the drinks arrived Midnight was deep in conversation with one of the hostesses. Madame Chow put the glasses down on the counter. With a bit of an effort Dave managed to pick three of them up at once. He took them back to the others.

'I see Midnight's well away,' he said. Good thing too, he thought. A quick bunk-up with one of Madame Chow's girls and he'd soon have forgotten all about his fiancée. *Ex*-fiancée.

'All right for the young and single,' Tony said, but when one of the girls came over and started stroking his hair, he didn't object.

Dave sat down. 'Any more like you at home, love?' he asked.

The girl giggled. 'Look behind you,' she said in bad English.

Dave turned round. Two more hostesses were coming over. One knelt down next to him. She stroked his arm, then his hair. He found himself wondering what she was – or wasn't – wearing under her filmy blouse.

He let himself sink a bit further into the cushions. Paddy and Tony were getting the same treatment, but Paddy looked distinctly uncomfortable and Tony was actually sitting up and didn't look at all pissed. Probably chucked his special into the nearest plant pot, Dave thought. Well, more fool him.

'See this man,' Tony said. He reached down from behind Dave and pinched his cheeks. 'This man is the rising star of the Junior NCO cadre.'

Dave's hostess looked at him blankly. Any minute

now, he thought, any minute now I am gonna have to do something about that blouse . . . to distract himself, he said, 'Well, once Dave Tucker decides to do something, there's no stopping him – '

The girl looked properly impressed. She put her finger to his lip. 'You very good,' she said. He touched her fingertip with his tongue and tasted lemon and tobacco. The girl moved a bit in the right direction – closer to him. It gave him a good view of the bar.

'Hey,' he said, realising Midnight was nowhere in sight. 'Where's heartbreak Horace gone?'

'You mean you have to ask, Dave?' Tony said.

'Well, now you come to mention it,' Dave said. He wondered how much a trip upstairs would cost. The way he felt, it would be good value even if it cost a month's pay. Specially considering the bad time Donna had been giving him.

He stood up. 'Just going to the bog,' he said. He licked his lips. 'Then upstairs. You know.'

Tony and Paddy exchanged glances. 'Off you go then, mate,' Paddy said. He didn't show any sign of moving. Neither did Tony.

In the bog, Dave discovered a problem. He went out as far as the door that led to the hallway. Tony was there, collecting his jacket. Dave leaned on the door jamb.

'Tone,' he said. A hostess in a peacock-blue silk dress pushed past. He watched her go appreciatively, then said, 'I haven't got any johnnies, and the machine is empty.' He announced it like the major disaster it was.

'What you looking at me for,' Tony said. 'Joy's on the coil.' He started to walk away.

Dave grabbed his tee-shirt. 'Where you going?'

'Home.' Tony looked pointedly at his watch. 'Joy gets the right hump if I'm much later.'

Dave stared at him, totally appalled. 'You can't go home yet – ' Another hostess went by. 'Look at that,' Dave said. 'We haven't got to the best bit yet.'

Tony stared at him. 'This ain't the best bit, mate.' Dave realized he was a lot more pissed than he was letting on. 'The best bit's at home, which is where I'm going and you should be going, and he should be going too – ' he pointed at Paddy, who had passed out on the sofa, ' – sleeping beauty over there.'

He shook Dave's arm off and went to get his jacket.

'Go on then,' Dave said to his back. 'All the more for us, you miserable old fart.'

He ambled over to Paddy and shook him. No response. 'Paddy,' he shouted. He put his finger on his mate's nose. Still nothing. 'Wake up, you prat.' Paddy opened his eyes and stared at him blearily. 'We're going for some rumpy-pumpy,' he said. Paddy waved an arm around until his hand connected with Dave's ear. He stroked it gently. 'Not with me, you pranny,' Dave said.

'Rumpy-pumpy pumpy-rumpy,' Paddy said.

'That's more like it, my old mate,' Dave said.

Paddy grinned and waved his other hand in the air. 'Yayy!' he shouted, and rolled off the sofa.

'No stamina, that's your trouble,' Dave muttered.

It was probably something to do with being an NCO. Maybe they put bromide in your tea or something. Well, he said to himself, all the more reason to make the most of it while I can. He went off in search of a suitable hostess. Any one would do.

And she did very nicely, especially after she stopped walking all over his back and started giving him the extras she'd promised.

A bit later, Dave paid up and decided he'd better be getting back. With a bit of luck it was so late he'd be able to sneak in without Donna noticing, even if he did have to sleep on the sofa.

Of course, the big problem was Paddy. Only one thing for it. Dave hoisted him up across his shoulders. 'Did you have to be such a big bastard?' he asked him. Paddy groaned. 'Just as well I'm a toughie,' Dave said. He staggered past the screen, towards the door.

Then he heard a voice he recognized. He looked across. Nancy was sitting on the sofa talking to Madame Chow. She was in uniform and she had a clipboard out. She turned round. He scuttled back behind the screen just in time. Paddy moaned.

There was a military policeman standing by the outer door next to the greeter. Only one thing for it, Dave decided. He waited till Nancy was deep in conversation, then made a dash for it. The MP wasn't the brightest thing in uniform, and he got in Dave's way.

Dave edged round him. The man stared at him.

'Bad flatulence,' Dave said, praying Nancy wouldn't hear him. Luckily, just at that moment Madame Chow tried to bribe her, and Dave got clean away.

He didn't go far though – Paddy was just a bit too heavy. He found an alleyway nearby and dumped him in it, next to some wicker baskets and a pile of old bits of timber. The place stank of rotten fish and cats' pee, but Dave didn't care. Nothing could make him feel worse than he did already.

He sat down next to Paddy, who slowly slumped over to lean on him. Dave stared at him. The blond Corporal looked about as good as Dave felt.

Tap water? Dave thought. That secret ingredient of Madame Chow's must have been more like nitro-glycerine.

He tore a bit of wicker off one of the baskets and started to pull it apart to help him think. And as for the other business . . . well, maybe he shouldn't have. There was Donna to think about, after all. But it was a bit late for that now – the best he could hope for was that she didn't find out.

'Where are we?' Paddy whispered.

Well, Dave thought. No point suffering alone – especially not when he had a god-given opportunity to wind Paddy up. He made a derisive noise. 'Oh mate,' he said.

'What do you mean, "Oh mate"?' Paddy asked.

'You didn't half give it some, my son,' Dave said. He frayed the bit of wicker some more.

'Wha'?' Paddy asked.

'You got up to some wild things, boy,' Dave said. 'You really gave it some welly.'

'Oh no,' Paddy said. If anything he sounded worse now than when he first woke up. He ran both hands through his hair. 'Oh shit,' he said. A look of horror came over his face. 'Oh shit,' he said again.

Luckily for Dave, Paddy managed to get his head inside one of the baskets before he chucked up.

Chapter 12

Dave didn't dare go home. Not coming in pissed and this late after the row he'd had with Donna that morning. Instead, he snuck into the mess hall and kipped on one of the settees in the recreation-room. There would have been hell to pay if he hadn't got out before people came in, but the sun streaming through the window woke him at dawn. He went off and sat by the waterfront till it was late enough so he could wander in without causing a stir.

He asked Paddy if he could sleep at his place that night, but the Corporal came on like a marriage counsellor – told him to sort himself out before he had to start classroom training on Monday.

Tony said the same, only louder.

That was all very well, but he knew for a fact Donna would just have a fit if he went back too soon. All he could do was make the best of it and hope not too many people noticed. That meant keeping his head down – long walks and solitary drinks in civvie bars – so it wasn't surprising that he didn't miss Midnight till he walked into the training-room all bright-eyed and bushy-tailed at six a.m. on the Monday morning. Then Dave realised he hadn't seen him since he disappeared at Madame Chow's. Oh well, he thought. At least *he's* got a clean uniform on.

Dave had known he was doing well when Mr Pereira – no more Paella-face, Dave had decided – made him cadre leader. He took up his position by the door. 'Right, you lot,' he bellowed to the class. 'Look lively. Berets off. Sit down and shut up.' Not that any of them weren't already doing it, like. But Dave liked the feeling of being in control – he was going to enjoy being an NCO, even a junior one.

He turned to Midnight. 'What happened to you on Friday night?' he whispered. After all, rank did have its privileges. Even if he didn't have a rank yet.

'I met someone.' Midnight grinned, almost shyly.

'Well, I figured that out,' he said.

'Yeah,' Midnight said, happily. 'We're getting married.'

'You wh – ' Dave exclaimed. A few heads turned to look at him. 'You what?' he hissed.

Midnight tapped Dave on the chest with his rolled-up beret. 'Tell you about her later,' he said, and went to sit down.

Dave heard an approaching footfall. 'Class!' he shouted, coming to attention, so did the others, where they sat in their seats.

Lieutenant Pereira came in. 'All present, sir,' Tucker said.

'Thank you, Tucker,' Pereira said. Dave went to his seat, near the front. 'Sit easy,' Pereira said, and the class relaxed. The Lieutenant went and stood in front of the blackboard. 'A whole week of lectures and written exams as part of your Junior NCO cadre, to include regimental customs and history, military law and the duties of an NCO.'

Nancy looked at him completely without sympathy. She pulled a sour face. 'Well, you're going to have to tell Donna,' she said.

'Oh yeah,' Dave said, thinking: Not bloody likely.

Nancy glared at him. 'She's pregnant, Dave –' As if I'm bloody likely to forget, he thought; but before he could say anything, Nancy said, 'This is very, very serious, Dave. If she's caught it –'

'I haven't been near her,' he said. 'Honest. We had a row – she threw me out –' She didn't believe him. He could see it all over her face. 'I haven't touched her,' he said quietly.

The trouble with being Dave the screw-up was that no one believed you even when you were telling the truth. All he could do was look straight at her and hope she'd decide to leave it to him.

'All right,' she said at last. 'Now, who else was with you?'

Oh shit, Dave thought. It just got worse. He hadn't thought it could possibly get worse. She'd never believe he'd gone on his own, and he couldn't think of what else to say.

'Who else was with you, Dave?' she demanded.

He stared at her. Her eyes went wide, and then he didn't need to say anything else because she'd figured it out for herself.

Donna was in bed by the time Dave got up the courage to go home. He was terrified of seeing Donna – terrified of what she might have heard, or what he might blurt out – but he couldn't stand the thought of another night on the rec-room couch.

The bedroom was in darkness, and Donna merely a long shape in the bed picked out by the moonlight shafting through the cracks between the closed curtains. He wanted to wake her up – to tell her that he really did love her, and if he didn't always show it – if he sometimes screwed up like everyone was always telling him – then that was his fault, not hers. But they always made up after a row by making love: the louder the row, the better the sex, Donna said. And not only was he not allowed to do that, he was so sore that the very thought of her touching him made him wince.

He undressed quickly, with his back to the bed, and slipped between the covers – carefully, so as not to let them touch him where he hurt – before she woke up.

He lay with his back to her, staring at the wall, wondering what she would say in the morning. He wouldn't be able to hide it from her for ever, that was for sure. And Paddy was going to be well pissed off with him when he realized who had landed him in it.

'Dave.' Oh shit, he thought. She's woken up. 'Dave,' Donna whispered again.

'I'm asleep,' he muttered.

'You do still fancy us, don't you?' She sounded really unhappy.

'Yeah,' he said, wishing he could roll over and prove it.

'I know I've put on a bit of weight recently,' she said, 'but you do still want us, don't you?'

'Look, I've got to get me sleep,' he said. 'I'm in the

Tony came back with his tail between his legs. Before Dave could say anything, Paddy stood up. 'I don't believe it,' he said in an awed voice.

Dave moved so he could see what Paddy was looking at. Midnight was coming through the door, hand in hand with a beautiful oriental girl.

'She's one of them hookers from Madame Chow's,' Nancy hissed.

Midnight either didn't hear her or ignored it. He went over to the table where Joy and Nancy were sitting. 'Ladies,' he said, 'I don't think you've met my fiancée.' He turned to the girl. 'Carmita,' he said. 'I'd like you to meet Nancy and Joy.' They stared at her blankly, not even bothering to try and raise a smile. The girl smiled shyly and sat down, making her mane of blue-black hair bob. Midnight said, 'I'll get you a drink.' He stuck a cigarette in his mouth and sauntered over to the bar. It was obvious that he knew he was the centre of attention, and that he was waiting for someone to make something of it.

What the hell do you say in a situation like this, Dave wondered. He decided keeping shtum would be the best policy.

Midnight leaned across the counter. He clicked his fingers at the barman. 'Two Scotches,' he said loudly.

Tony, being a Sergeant, felt he had to say something. Or maybe it was just because he was Tony. 'Oy! What do you think you're doing?' he demanded.

'What do you mean,' Midnight said around his cigarette. He lit up.

'You can't bring her here,' Tony said. He was

beginning to get agitated, and when Tony got agitated things generally got messy immediately afterwards.

'Why not?' Midnight asked.

Paddy leaned across Tony's shoulder. 'This is where the wives come, Midnight,' he whispered urgently.

Midnight rounded on him. 'So?' he demanded.

'So she works at Madame Chow's,' Tony said, in the voice he usually used on duty when he wanted to give someone a real bollocking but couldn't because there was an officer present.

Midnight squared off against him.

'Yeah,' Midnight said. 'And you really put the boot in, didn't you?' He took the cigarette out of his mouth. 'You told Fortune.'

'No,' Tony said. 'I told Pereira.'

'Yeah,' Midnight said. He slapped Tony lightly on the arm. 'Thanks a lot, mate.'

'I had to,' Tony said. It was true. They all knew that he would have an easier life if he did what the other senior NCOs did, and stopped mixing with the Privates.

'I confided in you.' Midnight sounded genuinely upset. Dave knew that would upset Tony more than any amount of shouting Midnight could do. He moved round a bit, to where he could grab hold of Midnight if it came to a fight. Paddy would have to handle Tony, but then he'd done that before.

Sure enough, Tony'd gone white with anger. 'Midnight,' he said through clenched teeth, 'She's a whore.'

232

Midnight grabbed the front of Tony's shirt and rammed him back into the bar. He had a good four inches more in height, and maybe twenty pounds in weight, and he held him there easily. Paddy moved to intervene, but Tony pushed him back. 'Leave it,' he said. He stared at Midnight, and for a second Dave couldn't tell which one of them was the angriest. 'Get your hands off me,' Tony said. 'Now.'

Midnight didn't move for what felt like a good fifteen seconds. Any second now Tony's going to have to do something about it, Dave thought. But then Midnight sneered and let go. He walked away. Tony flicked imaginary dirt off his shirt front.

For a minute Dave thought he was going to go for Midnight. 'He didn't mean it,' he said, trying to get himself between the two.

Midnight kicked a chair out of his way. They all turned to look at him. He spread his arms wide. 'The army don't own me,' he shouted. 'I can marry who I like.'

That you can, my old son, Dave thought. You just won't be in the army for very long afterwards.

Dave had hoped it would have all blown over by the next day, but Midnight skidded in only just ahead of Mr Pereira, and the way he sat to attention was only just this side of total insolence.

Luckily for Midnight, the Lieutenant chose to ignore him. He stood in front of the blackboard and read out what he'd written there. 'Military law – ' he started. Midnight dropped his biro on the desk, loudly. Pereira looked in his direction, but carried on speaking, ' – and how to formulate a charge.'

Before he could get any further, Midnight stood up. He pushed past the others in his row and ambled towards the door. Lieutenant Pereira stared at him for a second, and then said, 'Rawlings!' Midnight didn't stop. 'Where do you think you're going?'

Midnight came to a halt near the door. 'To the bog. I've got – ' he looked round, like he was a kid at school trying to get the other kids to laugh, 'gut ache.' Nobody did.

Dave couldn't watch. It was the kind of trick he used to get up to – wait till everything was going fine, find something to knock you off your perch and then stick two fingers up at everyone like it was their fault. Well, that was okay if you were a screw-up anyway, but he'd thought Midnight had better sense.

'Well, you don't just leave, Rawlings – you ask permission first,' Pereira said, managing to sound more like a nursery-school teacher talking to a naughty toddler than a CO talking to a soldier.

Bad move, Dave thought. He knew Pereira was probably just trying to give Midnight room to back down, but it would only bring out the worst in him.

He was right. Midnight put his hand in the air. 'Can I go to the bog. Please,' he said in a silly, high-pitched schoolboy voice. He paused, just half a second too long. 'Sir.'

'This kind of insolence will get you nowhere,' Pereira said quietly. Anyone else would have blown Rawlings's head off.

'I don't know what you mean, sir,' Midnight said in the same silly voice.

Pereira finally snapped. 'Well then I suggest you work it out. Sharpish.'

Midnight clicked his fingers at Pereira. 'Can I ask you something, sir? It's to do with military law.' He didn't wait for an answer. 'Why is the army so against blacks marrying orientals?' He turned to the class. 'Are they scared there'll be an uprising?' Christ, Dave thought. He'd heard of people burning their bridges, but Midnight had just done the equivalent of blowing up the Forth Bridge. 'Sir,' Midnight said. He made even that sound like an insult.

Pereira gazed levelly at him. 'Okay,' he said. 'Go.' Midnight headed towards the door. 'And don't bother coming back,' Pereira said. Midnight laid his head against the door. For one second Dave thought he'd seen sense. 'I'll see you in my office at sixteen-thirty hours,' Pereira said. 'Between now and then I'd suggest you get your attitude sorted out.' Only his last few words betrayed how angry he was. 'Get out.'

Midnight punched the door open. It slammed against the wall and he left.

Dave tossed his pen on the desk and put his head in his hands. 'That's it,' he moaned softly to himself. 'He's just blown his bloody stripe.'

Chapter 14

It seemed it wasn't only Dave who could fall in a cess-pit and come up smelling of roses. There was no other way to account for Midnight's presence in the Land-Rover taking them to the start point for their final test. Not that he seemed to appreciate his luck.

Well, he'd learn, Dave thought. The only question was how long it would take him. He leant back against the side of the Land-Rover and listened to the sounds of the jungle. There wasn't much else to do – they'd been blindfolded when they left the base. He'd been determined to try and figure out where they'd been taken, but he'd lost count of the twists and turns after the first half-dozen or so. Besides, they must have been driving round in circles for part of the time – they'd been going long enough to get to the Great Wall of China, or so it felt to Dave. All he was really certain of was that they'd crossed the bay – the sounds and smell of the harbour had been unmis-takable. Whatever they were going to do, it wouldn't be a regular training exercise – they'd been told to wear civvies.

The Land-Rover lurched to a halt. 'All right, div-vies,' he heard Paddy shout. 'Blindfolds off and let's have you out the lannie. Line up in three ranks.' He clapped his hands. 'Chop chop.'

Dave ripped his blindfold off. He blinked in the sunlight, then squinted at Midnight. If there hadn't been a Corporal with them on the ride, he was certain Midnight would have at least peeked, if not taken his off altogether.

And they have to partner us together, he thought. Well, it just went with the rest of the rotten luck he'd had recently. But it could be worse – at least most of the pain had gone now.

Dave jumped out, followed by most of the others. Midnight brought up the rear. 'Come on – do you want a stripe or not?' Paddy said.

Stupid question, Dave thought. Paddy caught hold of his jacket sleeve as he went past. 'Get through this one and you're home and dry,' he said. He whacked Dave gently on the shoulder. 'Good luck – go for it.' Dave nodded, and headed over to where the others were forming ranks on a bit of sandy ground between some lorries and a first-aid tent. Paddy caught his arm. 'By the way, I hear Rawlings blew it.'

Dave just looked at him and sighed. There wasn't the need to say any more. He turned and caught up with the others. Just in time. Instead of ordering them to attention, Tony yelled, 'Settle down, shut up and look this way.'

Hurriedly, the squad formed up and came to attention. None of them wanted to be the first to take advantage of Tony's informality.

Lieutenant Pereira strode out in front of them. 'Escape and evasion,' he said. 'Your objective – to get to Stanley Fort by eighteen hundred hours tomorrow,

237

avoiding capture by the enemy force. You'll perform certain duties *en route*.' He paused and looked at a piece of paper. As soon as he looked away, Midnight chomped on his gum – Dave couldn't help noticing, even in his peripheral vision. Bloody idiot, he thought. Don't know why they don't chuck him out of the cadre and put him out of his misery. And mine. 'One, collect a buffalo horn.' What the bloody hell, Dave thought. More like a kid's game than a training exercise. 'Two, a Marine's hat,' the Lieutenant went on. 'Three, a pair of the CO's boxer shorts.' There were a few hastily stifled snickers from behind Dave, and even the Lieutenant allowed himself a small smile. 'You will be pursued, and if you're caught you'll be made to start again. He paused. 'Now I know that some of these tasks are a bit daft – ' he actually sounded a bit embarrassed about it, and Dave really couldn't blame him. The Old Man's boxer shorts! ' – but this is a serious test of your ingenuity and initiative. Any questions?' Yeah, Dave thought. Do I really have to try and get through this with a bloke who's so keen he's been chewing gum on the sly all the time you've been speaking? But he didn't say anything. 'Fine,' Pereira said, looking straight at Dave. 'Good luck, and I hope you all do well.'

'Right,' Paddy said. 'Everybody into the tent for a strip search.' He grinned wolfishly.

Dave decided to take the most direct route possible – straight up and over the shoulder of the mountain.

They'd been supplied with a map, a compass and a canteen of water each and nothing else, but it should be enough to keep them from getting totally lost.

As he explained to Midnight, most of the others would probably choose the easier route, following the road. With a bit of luck most of the enemy would be tied up following them. By striking off on their own they would at least avoid the number of people they had to evade.

Midnight had just grunted, but at least he'd followed along.

That was why, an hour after the start they were clambering up a steep-sided hill. The air was bright and clear, and even the humidity wasn't too bad. This high up the land was less sodden, so it even smelt better – spicy, with a hint of something citrus. Pity there isn't time to enjoy it, he thought.

He fell flat as soon as he got to the top, to avoid being sky-lined – he wouldn't have come this far up at all, but he needed to get his bearings. Midnight clambered slowly up behind him, then just stood there, glugging on the water bottle. Dave grabbed him and tried to pull him down. The man was as solid as a rock. To hell with it then, Dave thought. He scrambled to his feet – if they spotted Midnight, he'd rather be ready to run than caught on his belly. And at least this way he'd get a better sighting.

'I reckon we should move by night – pick a route that has plenty of cover.' He suddenly realized that Midnight was still knocking back the water. 'Save that,' he said. 'You might need it.'

Midnight stared at him for a second, then spat the mouthful out so that it fountained on to the ground. Dave pursed his lips, determined not to say anything that would cause a row; but he suddenly realized how Pereira must have felt the other day in the training-room when Midnight had acted up – and how other officers must have sometimes felt about him over the years. Well, he thought, live and learn.

He studied the map. Midnight flicked it with the back of his hand, almost knocking it to the floor. 'You don't believe all that crap, do you?'

Dave sighed. 'What crap?'

'You don't really believe they're going to send an enemy force after us, do you?' His voice almost had that insolent little-boy quality he'd used on Pereira.

Much more of this and I'll whack him one, Dave thought. So help me, I will. 'Yeah,' he said. 'I do.'

He felt Midnight's fingers jab him in the temple. 'Bang bang,' he said, still in his kid's voice. He pushed Dave's head hard. 'You're dead.' Dave didn't react. Midnight shoved his face close to his. 'It's a joke,' he said.

Count to ten, Tucker, Dave told himself. He got to three before he threw the map to the ground, whirled round and grabbed Midnight's jacket. He glared up at the other man, not giving a damn for the difference in size. 'Listen, Midnight, I know you've had a run-in with the army, but you'd better not blow this for me.' He took a deep breath. 'Or I'll have you. You got it?'

Midnight just stared at him. His breath stank of the spearmint gum he was chewing. God knows where he'd hidden that, Dave thought. Like everything else about Midnight at the moment, it disgusted him. He shoved the man away. Then he picked up the map and walked away across the hillside.

He couldn't even be bothered to look back and see if Midnight was following him.

They were doing all right now, Dave thought. He'd found that the trick to keeping Midnight quiet was to keep moving, and he'd done just that, despite his earlier idea to move by night. But now he was just about done in. He knew he had to make sure they paced themselves. Ahead of them the broken scrub they'd been moving through gave way to an expanse of open ground. There was plenty of cover on the other side, but if they got caught in the middle they were done for – and knackered as they were, he didn't think they could outrun a bunch of old-age pensioners, let alone the rest of Number 1 Platoon.

He found a clump of bushes that offered reasonable cover while still letting him see what was coming. He knew it was useless to depend on Midnight – the lad was nothing but a dead weight. But one Dave was determined wouldn't drag him down.

'Okay,' he said breathing hard. 'We stop here for a bit.' He squatted down and took a swig from his canteen. Midnight sat down beside him. When Dave handed him the canteen, he hesitated until Dave virtually pushed it into his hand. He took a long drink. Spit it out and I'll kill you, Dave thought.

But Midnight just sat holding the canteen. 'I'm going to buy myself out,' he said quietly after a while.

It took Dave a couple of seconds to react – he could hardly believe what he'd just heard. 'You're what!' he whispered at last.

'I'm going to buy myself out,' Midnight said in his normal loud voice.

'Shut up,' Dave hissed. The enemy could be anywhere, and he didn't care how miserable Midnight was, he wasn't going to get sent back to the start – or worse, not get his stripe at all – for him.

'As soon as I get back,' Midnight went on. He still wasn't whispering. 'There's no point in staying on, is there? Not now.'

It was the stupidest thing Dave had ever heard. It wasn't as if Midnight had family on civvy street – he'd been brought up in a children's home, just like Dave had himself. 'You can't buy yourself out – you signed up for three years, you daft git. You haven't done half that.'

Midnight picked up a stone and hurled it as hard as he could. It hit a bush with a rattle that sounded as loud as gunfire in the quiet of the night. 'I'll get myself kicked out then,' he snarled.

Dave had had enough. In one movement he turned and launched himself at Midnight. Before the other man could react, Dave had grabbed his face in his hands. He took a couple of deep breaths. For a second he was ready to kill Midnight, or at least have a good go at it. 'Jesus Christ, what do you think you're playing at!' He slapped Midnight's face – not hard, just enough to really get his attention. 'Look, Midnight, I know how you feel – ' he did, but he

242

couldn't put it into words. He pushed Midnight away from him. 'Getting married,' he said, completely unable to hide his disgust. Midnight put his head in his hands. 'Yeah well,' Dave said, 'blokes like you and me, we need that . . .' He meant that they needed to find a place – a person – to belong to, because they'd grown up kicked from pillar to post in one children's home after another. He knew for a fact it was why he'd married Donna. Not that he regretted it. Not really. Not often. But that was different. He had to try and make Midnight see sense, and he just couldn't find the words to explain something so complicated. But the army – that was simple. They both understood the army. Or at least they had, until Midnight had met Madame Chow's little bit of jail-bait. 'The way you're going, you won't have anything,' he hissed, trying to keep an eye out for pursuers at the same time. 'Women,' he said. 'They can let you down, pal.' Midnight looked at him as if he were talking rubbish. 'Yeah, but your mates – your real mates never will.' He stopped, wondering if he really meant that – if he really meant Donna had let him down. But it didn't matter. What mattered was persuading Midnight. 'We're your real family, Midnight.'

'Look – ' Midnight said. He finally seemed ready to talk.

But just at that moment Dave heard something. It could have been an animal – a wildcat or a fox – but it sounded like a footfall. 'Shh!' he said urgently. He looked round. There were lights in the distance. He leapt to his feet. 'Come on,' he said. He ran a few paces, then realized Midnight wasn't following. He turned. Midnight spat out his gum, but still didn't get up. 'Come on, Midnight,' he said. The glow in the distance resolved into a line of men with lights, silhouetted against the night sky. 'It's them,' Dave hissed. Midnight looked round. Something galvanized him. He sprang to his feet.

They ran.

They lost the pursuit in the thick woods, and eventually Dave decided that they would have to sleep for a bit, but only if they took turns on watch. Midnight agreed less reluctantly than Dave had expected.

They moved on again at first light. Dave felt a bit the worse for wear, but it wasn't really that much worse than kipping on the couches in the rec-room. Prepare for life in the army. Get married, he thought gloomily.

Still, Donna was a problem for tomorrow. For now he had to figure out how to get the items on the list. A visit to the market seemed like a good bet for the buffalo horn — he'd seen them hanging up on market stalls there. God knows what the Chinese used them for — he'd heard a rumour that they ground them up and put them in their tea when the old sex life needed a bit of a boost.

Anyway, the market was almost on the way to the ferry, so they wouldn't lose anything by trying there.

They got to the market about mid-morning. The

smell of the fruit reminded Dave that he hadn't eaten in almost a day, and the water was long since gone. But it was the smell of the coffee from the pavement cafés that really threatened his sanity. All the more reason to get this over with and get back to base, he told himself firmly.

He led Midnight down an alley between two rows of stalls. On one side a fruit stall piled high with melons, bananas, apples, and a lot of other things Dave didn't dare look at, displayed its wares between a carpet salesman and a jeweller's selling pretty bits of glass pretending to be gemstones. Dave wished he had just a little bit of cash to buy a peace offering for Donna, but they'd taken away every last dollar.

He caught a whiff of musky, congealing blood, and realized there was a butcher opposite the fruit stall. He glanced over. There, hanging up among the fly-blown carcasses and joints, were a couple of buffalo horns.

'Buffalo horns!' he hissed at Midnight. He gestured at the crossroads ahead. 'Get over there and do your break dancing.'

'What?' Midnight said. He'd stopped complaining, but he still wasn't quite on the ball.

'Create a diversion,' Dave insisted. He shoved Midnight in the direction of the crossroads. 'Go on,' he said, 'just do it.'

Midnight looked blankly at Dave, but he went off obediently enough. Dave watched. Midnight just stood there in the middle of the road. Dave made a few half-hearted moves of his own to give him the idea. Then it seemed to take hold with a vengeance. Midnight clapped his hands a couple of times, then started a rap, 'I'm a rapper like M.C. Hammer.' He made a few moves, finishing up with a little twirl 'My name's Midnight, but it does not matter.' He clapped his hands a couple of times more. Dave was gratified to see a crowd beginning to form, including some of the stall-holders ... including the butcher. 'Carmita loves me – ' Might have known she'd come into it somewhere, Dave thought disgustedly. He started a slow drift in the direction of the butcher's stall. Everyone was watching Midnight now, and a few people were even beginning to clap along in time. One born every minute, Dave thought. 'And I love her,' Midnight sang. 'And I love her, be da be bong – ' Dave grabbed a buffalo horn. He held it behind his back, hidden in his clasped hands. Midnight was deep into his rap now, and didn't see him. 'Cor this market really pongs – but not as bad as Tucker's tummy – ' Charming, Dave thought. He realized there was only one way to get Midnight back. He started to dance a bit, and made sure he ended up near him. 'Specially when he's had a Ruby Murray.' Dave grinned. He held the horn up for Midnight to see, not caring who knew he had it now – they'd never be able to prove where he got it from – then danced on his way.

But not Midnight. He ran out of ideas, but he didn't let that stop him. He started singing a rock song Dave recognized but could not name, and went off into a really wild bit of break dancing.

Dave turned back, grabbed him by the sleeve and hauled him off, to the delight and applause of the crowd.

'Should have got the Marine's hat first,' Dave muttered. 'Then we could have put it down for a collection plate.'

He set off for the ferry. He wasn't quite sure where to find a Marine, but he was pretty certain they were more likely to be across the bay than here.

There was a problem: they didn't have the money for the ferry. Not to worry, he thought. They'd just have to hitch a lift. Of course, usually when you hitchhiked the driver knew he'd picked you up, but he reckoned what the ferry pilot didn't know couldn't hurt him. It was all going to be down to timing.

The only trouble was, there were an awful lot of people around. Dave strolled up to the ferry office, then straight past it, as if he were waiting to meet someone. The crowds began to thin out, and he knew that any minute now someone would ask if he wanted to buy a ticket. He spotted a pile of cleaning gear near the wall and wandered over to it. When the coast was clear, he squatted down behind it. He clutched the precious buffalo horn and settled down to wait – they couldn't jump aboard the ferry till the very last minute.

Time, Dave thought after a while. 'Just do as I do,' he said. He stood up and strolled as rapidly as he could down the colonnade towards the slipway. Midnight followed at his usual amble. 'Come on, Midnight, ' Dave hissed. 'The boat.'

He turned and walked down the slipway. It was only when he got to the bottom that he realized that Midnight had stopped following him. He looked up. Midnight was standing by the railing of the esplanade.

'I'm not going,' he said. Dave looked up at him, thunderstruck.

'What?' he demanded.

'I'm not going back,' Midnight repeated. He jerked his thumb in the general direction of the market. 'I'm choosing her,' he said.

'Midnight, don't be a prat,' Dave said. The whole idea was so ridiculous he couldn't even lose his temper over it.

'Well, who wants a bleeding stripe anyway,' Midnight said.

That did it. 'I do,' Dave shouted. He felt his face flush. 'Just because you blew it there's no need to louse it up for me,' he screamed. 'Midnight, you blew it the minute you walked out of the classroom – ' He felt as if he was going to explode. Couldn't the stupid pranny see how she was using him? What he was going to lose?

He suddenly realized that the ferry's rope had been cast off.

'Then there's no point in me carrying on, is there?' Midnight said. He seemed quite calm.

The ferry slipped quietly away from the jetty. 'Midnight!' Dave screamed. But it was no use. He'd gone.

Dave stared at his retreating back for a moment longer. Then he ran to the end of the jetty and jumped aboard the ferry. Soon he couldn't see Midnight at all.

His luck was in when he got to the other side of the bay. A squad of Marines were checking manifests. He wandered over to the one that was built least like a brick shithouse. He had a horrible feeling he was about to find out whether or not their reputation for extreme violence was just a myth.

'Afternoon,' he said. The Marine stopped checking things off on his clipboard and looked up. 'What a nice beret,' Dave said. 'Can I have it?'

The Marine didn't need to say anything. The look on his face said it all. Dave grinned like a looney and wandered off. There was another Marine nearby. They certainly liked their clipboards, the Marines – at least, this one was deeply interested in his. More to the point, his beret was rolled up under his shoulder tab.

Dave strolled over to him and, without saying a word, swiped it. The man didn't react.

Yes! he thought. And clean away with it, too. Dave walked away backwards, holding it behind his back. He was ready to run if he had to, but he didn't think he would. The stupid Marine hadn't noticed a damn thing.

He turned round and found himself facing two of the biggest Marines he'd ever seen. He smiled. He shrugged. They weren't impressed. He walked rapidly back to the Marine he'd nicked the beret off. He tapped the man on the shoulder and handed his beret back without a word. He smiled at the other two Marines.

They weren't impressed. One of them glanced at the other. Then they both looked first at Dave and then at the bay.

The two Marines advanced on him. He didn't even bother to make a fight of it, he just made sure he hung on to the buffalo horn. They picked him up.

Oh, not the water, he thought. Please not the water.

But it was all right. They threw him on to the rubbish dump instead.

After that, Dave decided discretion – as it applied to Marines – was the better part of valour. Maybe he'd say that he and Midnight had split up, and Midnight was supposed to get the Marine's hat. Or something.

That just left him with the Old Man's boxer shorts to collect. He got himself up to the Fortunes' house without any problems. It was a white bungalow that sprawled in acres of lawn and formal garden. There was a lovely long line of washing in the breeze, and no sign of the maid who had put it out. No gaps in it, either, so it looked like he was the first one back. He considered all sorts of devious routes across the stretch of lawn that separated him from his prize, but there wasn't any cover to speak of.

Then he thought, what the hell. The washing wasn't in line of sight of the house anyway. In the end, he just walked up and grabbed the first pair of boxer shorts he came too. He was about to go back the way he'd come when he heard a car pull up. He ran to the verandah of the house, then dropped to a crouch and ran along it, doing his best to keep under the line of the windows. He'd just made it to the safety of the bushes when the car pulled up and the Old Man and his wife got out. Dave hid behind the biggest yucca plant he could find. Mrs Fortune wandered over in Dave's direction while the Old Man got a bag out of the car. She peered at Dave for a moment, then wandered back to her husband.

Dave heard her say, 'Why's Tucker hiding behind our bush?'

Oh no, Dave thought. Not now. Not after all I've been through.

Colonel Fortune grinned. 'Just pretend you haven't noticed,' he said.

Dave made it back to base with ten minutes to spare. He knew he ought to go straight to Pereira and explain about Midnight, but he didn't. Instead he perched himself on the admin block steps and settled down to wait.

You couldn't write your friends off that easy. Not when they were your family. You had to give them every chance you could.

Paddy and Tony strolled up the road. They were laughing together. Bet they've made it up with Nancy and Joy, he thought. That was the next thing he'd have to do – come clean to Donna and ride out the explosion. He'd rather do that than have her go round thinking he didn't fancy her just because she was pregnant – it wasn't as if she'd been thrilled with the idea in the first place.

'Oy!' Tony said, suddenly all Sergeant. 'Where's Rawlings.'

'We . . . sort of lost each other,' Dave said. He wondered if they'd take his stripe away if Midnight didn't show and he didn't come clean about it. But that was okay. Some things were more important.

But then Paddy said, 'He did a bunk, right?' So that was Dave off the hook.

'Not exactly,' Dave said, suddenly despondent. He stared at the ground. Maybe he should have argued better – not lost his temper so quickly.

Tony checked his watch. 'You better see Pereira,' he said. 'Your time's nearly up.'

''Nother ten minutes yet,' Dave said. They all knew what he was waiting for.

'Don't be stupid, Dave,' Tony said. 'You don't want to blow it because of him.'

'He'll be here,' Dave said. It wasn't that he believed it, just that he had to give Midnight every chance there was.

Paddy slapped him on the back. 'You did it, Dave.' He whacked him lightly on the head. So did Tony, and suddenly they were both raining light little slaps on his head.

When they stopped he grinned up at them, suddenly proud of himself. 'Unbelievable,' Tony said as they left him.

He sat there holding the buffalo horn and the Old Man's boxer shorts for another couple of minutes. He was suddenly sure everything would be okay – him, Donna, the stripe. Only Midnight not being there took the edge off things. But it couldn't be helped.

He stood up, and took one last look at the road outside the gates. And there was Midnight, ambling along and chewing a wad of gum like it was the most natural thing in the world.

Dave went up to meet him. Without saying a word, Midnight held something out to Dave. It was a Marine beret.

'Where'd you get it?' Dave asked, incredulous.

'Off the punter that was screwing Carmita when I arrived,' Midnight said. He took a deep breath, and that was the only thing that let Dave know he was upset.

'The passport scam?' Dave asked.

'The passport,' Midnight agreed. 'Come on – we don't want to be late for Maradona, or he won't give you your stripe, will he?'

Together, they went inside.

Epilogue

It was hard to believe they'd been in Hong Kong the full two years. Harder still to believe that by the time they marched out there would be no more King's Own Fusiliers. But that was what the rumours that had been flying around camp all week said.

Now they were going to find out for sure. It was their Drumhead Service, the one that would see them out of Hong Kong, maybe the last one they would have anywhere. Everyone was there – men, officers and wives.

Dave stood at attention, wandering what the hell he was going to do if the regiment was disbanded. Paddy had already said he didn't want to be with another mob – that he'd leave if he came to it, maybe follow Nancy wherever she was posted now that she'd got her permanent RMPC rank. Dave didn't credit that – Paddy was army through and through, maybe even more so than Tony. And God only knew what Tony would do.

But himself – he didn't know. Donna would like it if he left, but what was there on civvie street for a dead-end kid with no qualifications who hadn't even really made a go of it inside? Nah – he'd stick around whatever happened.

The Old Man took his place next to the padre. He looked grim. It was his speech first, then the service. 'As we salute the Colours, we salute the men and women who died defending them,' he began. 'Protecting their country. Obeying orders. And this is one more order.' He paused. It was clear from his face that it wasn't an order he was going to enjoy giving, or one that he expected anyone to enjoy carrying out. But that wasn't the point, Dave thought. You did it anyway, because that was what being a soldier *was*. 'The Regiment of the King's Own Fusiliers is to be merged – ' So that's it then, Dave thought. No more *us*. ' - to form a new Midlands Regiment, along with the Cumbrians and the Rutlands . . .' He wondered how different it was going to be; and then it occurred to him that the Old Man might not even be part of the new order. 'It's happening all through the army. The Cold War is over, and our role worldwide is changing.' There was a long pause while they got used to it. Dave risked a glance sideways. Tony was getting well choked up. Paddy wasn't much better off. 'There's no reason why any of you should lose out from this,' the Old Man continued. 'The new regiment will need good people, and whatever you decide to do individually, you will always have pride that you were Fusiliers. The King's Men. The Best.' The Old Man smiled, but he was crying at the same time. Dave realized he was, too. 'But this is our Drumhead Service,' he concluded, 'so let's have a bloody good day, a bloody good pray – and then disperse and get bloody well plastered.'

And in the end, since there was nothing much else they could do, that was what they did.